It Is Solved By Walking

Helen Weston was born in St Helens, Lancashire in 1949. She studied English at Oxford and worked in adult education for many years, later training as a therapist. She has lived and worked in Finland and also spent five years in an Anglican convent before leaving and marrying her husband, an ex Benedictine abbot. Her memoir, *The Winter is Past*, describes those years. She is a founder member of Borderlines, Carlisle's book festival, and is also associated with Words by the Water in Keswick. She has two sons and continues to practise as a therapist in Cumbria.

Ambulando Solvitur: It is Solved by Walking

The original words were spoken in Greek by the philosopher Diogenes, when asked by Zeno to prove that motion was real. He uttered these words as he walked away. The Latin version was quoted by St Augustine of Hippo, to encourage perseverance.

Also by Helen Weston
The Winter is Past

It Is Solved By Walking

BY HELEN WESTON

Helen S. Weston

With love & best wishes

For Diana,
my guide on the journey underground

One

Dodo's house is a mid-terrace on one of the streets joining the Cowley Road to the Iffley Road, at the shabby end of Oxford. I have come as quickly as I could, but there is no way you can get from Penrith to Oxford in much less than four hours. I know she doesn't finish work till 4.30 on Fridays, but I can't help looking out for her as I pay off the taxi and retrieve the key from under the metal foot scraper.

Despite my trepidation, her house embraces me like an old friend. There are two small square rooms opened out into one big space, with windows at both ends, so that the light floods in. The walls are roughly plastered and painted white, like a Greek village house, and there are splashes of vibrant colour everywhere – Afghan rugs and cushions, Peruvian wall-hangings, silver-encrusted icons, a squashy teal-blue sofa, and of course bookcases squeezed into every available space.

The cushions and rugs were always pressed into service for exotic dens and palaces when I was young and the sofa was a place to squirrel away all my favourite novels and poetry books, which I could read in peace while Dodo wrote her travel articles.

There is a small stack of books tucked into the side of the sofa now and I can see with pleasure that we still share the same taste in novels, though I don't really get her new interest in Jungian psychology.

I can see at a glance the familiar tottering piles of CDs – the Beatles, Dylan, Leonard Cohen, Simon and Garfunkel, Neil Young,

Joni Mitchell. A few new ones like Fleet Foxes and Mumford and Sons but nothing too surprising. All singer-songwriters. The lyrics were always crucial to her.

She wasn't like a real aunt because of the small age gap (seventeen years) between us. She wasn't like a godmother either, because she was so independent and wild and out of the country more often than in it, but she was always there when I needed her, which is why I am here now. Her voice on the answer-phone asking me to come sounded very agitated.

Lunch is laid out for me in the kitchen, but not on the table, as it usually is. Lancashire cheese and a fresh Rye loaf are set out on the Shaker sideboard, next to a bowl of vine tomatoes and a bottle of Pinot Grigio. All my favourites, but there is something a bit staged about the way they are arranged. Dodo could not be accused of being neat.

On the battered oak table a cloth-bound book sits on its own in the middle, under a pool of light. It is a beautiful book that looks like a journal or something bought with a particular purpose in mind. There is sketch of a hare on the front, caught in mid-leap, with long, sinuous ears, quivering with energy. The lines are very spare and the colour just suggested in splashes of grey-green and rust. I can see her rifling through piles of possible notebooks until she spots the exact one.

There is a note lying next to it, held down by a kitchen knife. It is in Dodo's handwriting and simply says: 'Please read this, Meg. I need you to understand and I can't find a way to tell you face to face. I will come back on Sunday.'

She is the only one who calls me Meg. Every body else calls me Maggie, even Tom. Sometimes I think she is the keeper of my soul. I am scared of opening the book, in case it tells me something I don't want to know. Consequently I handle it warily, stroking the gold-tooled edges and admiring the thick, creamy paper.

A cursory flick through the contents reveals twenty chapters of closely written text, in her characteristic blue italic writing, with lots of rough drawings spread throughout the text. The pictures seem hastily drawn, as if it had been important to record something on the spot. Occasionally there is a Polaroid photograph slipped in between the pages.

It looks like a description of some esoteric process, carefully and minutely recorded over twenty meetings. There is no introduction at the start of the book, no explanation of what the process is. The first chapter goes straight into the first meeting, without any preamble, except for the line: 'This is an accurate record of what follows.'

My phone is beeping, with yet another message from Rachel, my sixth former who is stage-managing the school play. The set has collapsed and the art class are fighting each other and refusing to fix it. Last time it was about the text – could they change the ending to make it more believable? I tried to explain that you can't do that with Shakespeare, but they didn't see why. I can't think about it now.

I can't think about anything. I didn't give Tom much warning about my decision to drop everything and come, so he was pretty fed up, and the children were jarred by the suddenness of my departure, but it didn't feel as if I had a choice. Dodo's unexpected absence has made me feel completely deflated. Perhaps a walk will help. I certainly can't concentrate to read. Outside, it is cold and frost-bound, but the sun is bright and luring me out.

I set off down the Iffley Road and up the High to Merton Street, cutting through the cobbles to Christ Church Meadow so that I can get to the river. The winter sun lights up the Cotswold stone and the faces of the passers-by indiscriminately, making it all look as if it has been shot by Merchant Ivory. It is so cold that you can almost imagine the skating parties on the Thames/Isis in Victorian times.

There are still some hardy undergraduates doing their sculling practice, despite the hoar frost on the trees, and I watch them absently as I walk up the towpath towards Folly Bridge, trying to put myself in Dodo's shoes.

It is weird to think of her probably doing this walk on a regular basis. She studied at St Hilda's in the late sixties, I know, so I am returning to her old haunts by coming back to Iffley Road. I also remember her reminiscing about romantic assignations in Christ Church Meadow, on one of the college barges moored there, so it's an educated guess that this was her preferred route.

What was she thinking about as she scanned the river traffic and assessed the other regulars? What made her suddenly decide to leave me the journal and duck out of talking to me?

I thought I knew her better than anyone, but maybe it was all one way. There is the evidence of the carefully chosen novels and poetry she used to send me, timed to arrive at exactly the right stage of my life, and the travellers' tales with which she used to regale us all at Christmas and birthdays, with the pitch-perfect accents accompanying them, but what do I know about her inner life?

She has always been such a familiar part of my life that I can't imagine there being anything left for her to tell me, but there was clearly something so difficult that she couldn't raise it face to face. She could even have been mulling it over on this very towpath.

Maybe she has some terrible illness and is planning a trip to Dignitas, but why all those journal entries? She could just tell me straight.

It is all so disturbing that coffee seems a very welcome diversion. Coming through the Meadow gate onto Folly Bridge, I turn up St Aldates in the cold white air, heading for the coffee shop I remember half way up. Everything hangs in suspended life.

Even the constant passage of people on the street outside looks dreamlike as I warm my hands on the bowl of the cup and stare through the steamed-up windows at the college gardens opposite.

I can see her office from here. She never really wanted to work for a publisher of art books but it paid the bills and allowed her to indulge her passion for travel writing. The biggest part of the attraction was that it was almost opposite Christ Church, one of her favourite colleges.

She used to talk about her time as a student at St Hilda's, how she loved marching over Magdalen Bridge and up the High (you never called it the High Street) to go with her friends to some amazing lecture at the English Faculty building in St Cross. The everyday lecturers were celebrities – people like Dame Helen Gardner and Christopher Wordsworth.

Clearly she never stopped being dazzled by the place, never quite adjusted to the culture shock after her northern grammar school, but what she was really high on was beauty and the serious attention paid to it in all its forms. I think it had seemed like an indulgence when she was growing up, a secret vice. The worst thing you could be in her home-town in Lancashire was a *poser*. Mother told me the same – you would do anything to avoid it.

I know that after she left she was always trying to recapture that intensity – the *Brideshead* phenomenon. It's clear that lots of people stay on in Oxford long after they should have left because they haven't weaned themselves off it, but I get why they do, even if it doesn't fit my politics. Sometimes I think Dodo was my real mother. I wasn't meant to be the daughter of a maths teacher.

There is a handy bus when I reach the High, which transports me very quickly past the indoor market and Queens College down to Magdalen. I get off at the Plain, just the far side of the bridge, and walk up Iffley Road to the house. She would have been home by now, but there is no light on.

5

There is nothing for it but to start. I break off a piece of cheese and sit down at her big oak table, the site of so many exuberant and exotic meals, raising my glass to her as I open the book. We are straight into the first meeting.

1st Meeting – 16 October 2012

Arrived at Elinor's house exactly on time, only to discover it was the wrong day. Nearly gave up on the spot but she said she had a cancellation and I could come back in half an hour. Went to Stow and had a coffee there, then re-presented myself, feeling stupid.

It was a rambling old house on the edge of a village a few miles from Stow-on-the-Wold. The front garden had a square lawn with mature herbaceous borders only just held in check. A big back garden was visible through a gate in a high fence.

Elinor came out of a small annexe attached to the right side of the house and met me at the fence gate. She had clearly been watching for me. She was tall and willowy, as I remembered, but her expression was more reserved than it had been at the workshop the previous month. She was wearing a long velvet jacket in a rich dark turquoise, with a contrasting cobalt blue scarf, also in velvet. The outfit was flamboyant and arty and strangely at odds with her reserve. She smiled but said very little, guiding me through the open gate and closing it carefully behind us so that we were sealed off in our own private space.

You had to walk to the end of the garden to reach the hut, which was about the size of a large summerhouse. It was warm inside and there were two boxes of sand on raised stands at one end, with high stools facing each other across them. There was a big jug of water next to one of them. A tangy, resinous smell, like the inside of a sauna, permeated the space.

Round the walls, on two sides, were new-looking pine shelves almost from floor to ceiling, covered with small objects and figures.

They were grouped together according to type and the shelves arranged in ascending or descending order – maybe an evolutionary order, as the bottom shelf had things like shells and rocks and feathers and the top one had fantasy figures and wizards, wise women, buddhas, Virgin Mary statues, etc.

There were kings and queens, knights and soldiers, mothers and fathers, children, houses, furniture, as well as lighthouses, castles, compasses, scales, typewriters, emergency vehicles, birds and animals of every description. There was a basket to put your choices in.

It was all done in silence. You were supposed to pick up objects or figures you were instinctively drawn to. It was hard not to feel self-conscious. I was afraid of looking stupid or shallow – choosing predictable objects. You were supposed to choose spontaneously, override the inner censor, but how could you possibly do that?

Elinor had gone in before me and was sitting down on one of the stools, with her back to the window, waiting for me to bring over my choices and place them in the sand. Sitting there with her notebook and pen she looked elegant and rather intimidating, her greying hair caught up expertly in a tortoiseshell clip, and I was afraid that my unconscious would disappoint her and produce only clichés.

My palms were sweating and my brain was stuck in freeze mode. What were the right things to choose? My eyes skidded across the shelves – like the supermarket on a bad day.

Suddenly my hand reached out and picked up the hare and the crusader knight, then the lion and the mother-and-child. They were placed securely in the bottom of the basket. The hare and the lion and the crusader knight were all very lifelike, moulded in resin – probably from somewhere like the Early Learning Centre – and the mother-and-child were carved out of one piece of black soapstone, their outstretched hands joined to form a circle.

Having made my first risky choice, I was able to stand before the shelves and see what was on them. There was a sinuous coiled snake, still with some sand adhering to it. I liked the rubbery feel of it and the red eye and forked tongue and put it straight into the basket. Then, on the bottom shelf, there was a shiny brown-speckled shell in the shape of an egg. That went in too. Next I went for a house on one of the middle shelves but found myself hesitating over it, choosing instead a ceramic table with tiny loaves and mugs laid out on it.

I had what I wanted so took the basket to the sand tray and sat down on the stool opposite Elinor. The jug was within easy reach in case water was needed. I had no idea what was supposed to happen next, except that Elinor would probably not speak and I could do what I wanted with the figures and the sand.

Although she was sitting opposite, Elinor didn't look at me – there was no attempt to make eye contact. We were both looking at the sand, almost like waiting for a play to begin. I took all the figures out of the basket and grouped them round the middle of the sand, unsure of where to put them. I began to talk about the figures, but it wasn't talk like in a conversation: it was talking to myself – out loud like a child does. Elinor seemed to know that and only made a slight encouraging noise. She made a quick sketch but no words.

Talking to myself helped and I began to be clear that the lion and the knight should be further away from the middle, so moved them to the top left-hand corner. 'The knight used to be very important,' I said, 'but his power is fading, so he needs to be further away.'

I found myself coiling the snake around the shell, partly because they cried out to be connected and partly because they seemed a natural fit. The two of them gradually took central position in the tray with the mother-and-child on the left and the hare on the right. That felt right. But the table was important too. It was up against the back wall of the tray, in the middle, and had to stay there, though I didn't know why.

I realized that my fingers had been absently stroking the sand for some time and that minutes had passed, in which I had half-buried the knight. 'The figures feel very powerful,' I said.

Elinor murmured something about how the knight seemed less important now – not looking at me but observing the half-buried figure in the top left corner. She asked what he had meant for me.

I told her that when I was young I was always a tomboy, never did girly things, always wanted to build dens with my brother and his friends, play the boys' parts in the school plays. I was obsessed with the quest for the Holy Grail. Life had to be heroic and meaningful. I even had a picture of an Arthurian knight kneeling in an all-night vigil on my wall as a student (the 'Monty Python' version came later).

I looked up but Elinor didn't speak and it somehow seemed OK to carry on. I told her about this very vivid dream I had had just a few weeks ago in which I was in a deep underground cave, hopelessly lost in the dark. At my most desperate point I was saved by a crusader knight in chain mail and white tunic, walking in front of me and lighting the way with his sword held high in front of him.

'In Jungian terms, he was probably your animus, or inner masculine side,' she said. 'He was important to help you find a way out but he is not so important anymore. Is that right?'

'Yes. He brought me here but the things in the middle are the important ones now.'

I looked down at the figures grouped there and saw the vulnerability of the shell/egg and how it was so fiercely and closely protected by the snake coiled round it and said, 'I can't get rid of the knight yet, can I, because the egg is too vulnerable and needs protection?'

She shook her head and said, 'He's your armour perhaps, but the snake is also there and it carries the wisdom of the feminine.'

I found myself stroking the mother-and-child with a kind of longing, tears suddenly very close. 'I think my mother loved me as much as she could but I never felt she really "saw" me,' I said.

'Perhaps she saw your strength but not your need...'

The conversation subsided again, like water finding its own level. My attention turned to the table with the tiny loaves on it at the back of the sand tray and I built it up higher, using the water, talking to myself, as I adjusted the height.

'This is really important. It's a safe, stable place for all of us, but particularly for the children. It's important to maintain it, hold it together.'

'It's important to hold it together,' Elinor echoed.

I nodded and carried on with my construction work – it seemed unnecessary to speak. Eventually it was high enough and solid enough and I could leave it for a minute to look again at the shell and the snake. There was a really strong pull towards the centre but I said I was scared of what would happen if I neglected the table.

'What if you left the table to fend for itself?' Elinor said. 'How could you get to the centre?'

I picked up some stones from the bottom shelf behind me to try and create a path but it didn't seem to work. I reduced the height of the table to try and lessen its significance but it wasn't enough. 'I'm afraid of the shell cracking open,' I said.

'What is inside the shell?' Elinor said.

'Something really precious but so tightly wound in that if I let it out it will flood everything.'

'But do you want to let it out?'

'Oh yes.'

'Could the lion help?' she asked.

We both suddenly looked at the lion – still standing in the top left-hand corner near the half-buried knight. It didn't seem quite as important as the other figures and I thought I had perhaps chosen it too consciously – probably Aslan associations. I shook my head.

I looked at the hare – as close to the shell as the mother-and-child but on the other side – and wondered if that could provide an

answer. No, it had the creative power but it was a wild creature and
was only really there on sufferance.

Elinor said how beautiful the shell was – only found in deep waters
and a completely natural thing. She drew my attention to the egg
shape and wondered aloud if it needed a safe place to be born.
Her comment made me realize how safe I already felt in this
environment. I thought about the layers of containment round the
figures – the tray itself, Elinor's 'creative attention', the hut. It was
like watching the camera pan out from the sand – further out and
higher up until you were back in the ordinary world.

That seemed to be the point at which the session came to its
natural end. We both seemed to feel it at the same time and Elinor
lifted her head and looked at me: 'OK to stop?' When I nodded, she
took out her Polaroid camera and took a picture of the sand tray,

giving it to me as soon as it emerged. The clunky technology felt appropriate somehow, watching it slowly become clear. She led the way out of the hut and back to her house. I was reluctant to speak, as I still felt a long way down. We managed to put in another date and I left. The whole thing had taken barely an hour.

What *is* this process and why does Dodo want me to sift through it all with her? It is like watching somebody doing archaeology on their own heart – almost shockingly intimate.

And what about Elinor? Who was she? Was she paid to sit there? Was this some kind of therapy, and, if so, what was Dodo hoping to heal in herself?

Perhaps she was not as sorted as she had always appeared. All that stuff about the knight holding up the sword to light the way – what did that mean in real life? Was it something to do with allying herself with her father rather than her mother? I know very little about her father, my grandfather. He died when I was still small.

Then there is the table with the tiny loaves on it and her comment about holding it together for the children. What children?

If there are twenty of these sessions, how long is it going to take me to read it? If Dodo is coming back on Sunday, that means I've got at least a day, but I don't feel comfortable not knowing where it's all leading. Can I jump to the end, or is it cheating – like looking at the last page of a detective novel before you've worked it out?

Dodo was always very strict about not reading the end of the story till you'd read the rest. She would expect me to read it from beginning to end in the right order. I would almost go so far as to say that she left it for me to read because she knew I wouldn't jump the gun.

She would see it as a commitment – like walking a labyrinth where the twists and turns of the path are the whole point. You could easily just walk across the lines, but you would have learned nothing. There's a phrase our Latin teacher always used to quote, from St Augustine: '*Ambulando solvitur*. It is solved by walking'.

All the same, I have to look. Never liked my Latin teacher anyway.

It ends with the words: *I will do it once Christmas is over,* which seems to refer to speaking to me – perhaps giving me the journal itself. It is January now, start of the new term, so she's done that bit but I can't make sense of anything else just before that, so I am no further on.

Two

I know there will be answers in the journal but I need something more tangible. I feel like ransacking the house until I find the clue that will make sense of it all. Her mobile says unavailable. I head for the loft, muttering to myself as I mount the ladder.

I don't know what I'm looking for but in films it's always the loft where the secrets lie. In the event it's crammed with every conceivable bit of junk accumulated over a lifetime of travel and hoarding, but none of it seems hidden away. There are several bags of letters (some of them clearly love letters) in at least three different hands, financial files bursting out of ring binders, stacks of photo albums going back to schooldays, old trunks full of more-or-less vintage clothing, teetering piles of discarded LPs from the sixties and seventies, jewelled cushions made out of old saris, rolled-up CND posters, etc, etc.

Maybe there was too *much* life up there in the loft and she'd had enough. Perhaps something had suddenly made her ask what it was all for, something in those sessions with Elinor. She was always a beauty, with her dark hair and blue eyes, and those amazing cheekbones, but things had never quite worked out for her. Was it a man? But why was she telling *me*? Was there something she wanted from me? Had I disappointed her in some way?

I studied literature because I wanted to be like her but I always had the nagging feeling that she felt I had gone for the safe option by becoming a teacher – even though she knew I liked it. It was

Mother who exerted the pressure, but I capitulated pretty easily, stayed in my Northern stronghold. I could have left Lancaster, gone somewhere else for my teacher training, done some travelling, but I didn't. I met Tom, got married, had two kids. We were Thatcher's children. It was all about getting a career, buying our own place, making a success of our lives.

Dodo was always on the sidelines, holding out her hand, offering something else. Why didn't I take it? She offered to take me with her on a trip to Prague when it first opened up to the West and I didn't go because I had just met Tom. I still remember the look on her face when I turned her down, though she made light of it. I often had the feeling that there was some kind of sadness in her life, but she never let you near it, always deflected attention away from herself with a witty comment or one of her stories.

Tom thinks she comes too close, almost to the point of trying to get between us, but I think he's wrong. It's just that his family don't do closeness – particularly his mother.

My eye suddenly lights upon a disreputable dog on wheels, with scraggy fur and one blind eye, and I am transported back to all those happy summers when I was allowed to come and stay with Dodo while Mother was at her maths conferences in Oxford. I can't bear it if anything serious is wrong with her...

Perhaps the letters will shed some light. I empty out the first bag-full and begin sorting them into piles. There are a surprising number from Mother, who was at teacher training college when Dodo was a young teenager. I am not surprised to see that they are full of serious sisterly advice about working hard and not letting young men take advantage of her. It was the early sixties but Mother was clearly untouched by the emerging youth culture. It sounded like she and her friends were all good girls, carefully insulated from the outside world by the college authorities.

Of course there are none of Dodo's replies, though I can guess what they were like. She was just starting grammar school in the early sixties and the Beatles were bursting onto the music scene just fifteen miles from where she lived. She had a Saturday job in a local shop, so she had a bit of money. What was to stop her? Her mother of course. My mother told me what she was like – a real toughie, streetwise to the nth degree, brought up in hard conditions before the War then seasoned by her time in the WAAF where she met my grandfather.

I know they used to set curfews for my mother before she went to college. She had to be brought back to the door by half past ten or there would be trouble and boyfriends would be berated on the doorstep if they were five minutes late. My grandfather was a bit of a disciplinarian apparently – all those years in the RAF during the war had left him with clear ideas of what mattered. Was it the same for Dodo seven years later?

The sixties were her teenage years. Did they have the Pill? My mother said that even tampons were suspect in the mid-sixties where they lived and you still had to wear knickers both inside and outside your tights when they first came in. It certainly wasn't the King's Road.

How did Dodo cope? I open another bag of letters. This one looks more promising. Clearly she had a friend who had got away. Most of these are dated 1967 or 8, when she was in the sixth form, and are postmarked London. He was an art student at St Martins.

She must have somehow swung it with her parents to go down and visit him. Looks like there was a relation or someone she could stay with. She discovered Chelsea and had her first sighting of a Biba store. Her eyes were opened. It's clear from the letters that she slept with him, so she must have known about the Pill, or had some other form of contraception, because any possibility of an illegitimate child would have freaked out their mother.

However, it looks like he was her first love and she fell really hard.

Several letters from him at the bottom of the bag are attempting to extricate himself from the guilt of ending it:

'I'm sorry Dodo but I have to get out of England – you know how it is. I want to go to the Atlas Mountains and Marrakesh, Casablanca and all that stuff. I need colour and *life*. You will be alright. You have your scholarship. You will be able to make a clean start at Oxford without me.'

Hm... Those kinds of letters don't change, only the place names.

I've closed up the trapdoor into the loft for now, though the dog has come down with me. He's had a quick hoover and a face-wash and is happily sitting beside me at the table, where I can reach down and stroke him. Time for a coffee and another go at the journal.

I remember Dodo telling me years ago when I was still at school that if I kept a journal it needed to be written in a beautiful book – just like this one. She gave me one for my fifteenth birthday and said I must treat it with great respect. I still have it now, though there's not much in it.

I open the journal at the second meeting, looking briefly at the drawings again. They are pretty rubbish, which cheers me up for some reason.

2nd Meeting – 7 November 2012

Cold, but bright and sunny as I was driving over. The Cotswold hills were that beautiful smoky grey-green colour that always reminds me of Tuscany. Was anxious again about whether I had got the time right. Consequently arrived fifteen minutes early and had to sit outside and wait.

Don't know why I was so anxious about being late. Think I thought Elinor might be angry with me. Ridiculous at my age, I know, but it's the truth. Probably regression or something.

We sat in her little room in the annexe for the first quarter of an hour and I found it hard to talk – something about meeting her eyes.

Apparently this is what we do first – talk about anything that has come up before we go into the hut. I like the silence better – feels more contained.

Was able to tell her about the image of the taproot that had come to me when I was sitting in the dentist's waiting room last week. Was trying to calm my mind by meditating on the sand tray and had this strong sense of a taproot going down through the centre of the tray and finding water. She liked that.

I also showed her the labyrinth poem I had suddenly written a week after our session. Haven't written a poem for years. I think I was remembering the labyrinth in Grace Cathedral – the San Francisco one. She was particularly taken with the turn to the left at the start of the poem. Apparently the left is the way to the unconscious and you do need to go against the flow.

Just for the record, this is the poem:

Labyrinth
It can be pebbles or hedges
Lines in turf or low walls
It makes no difference
The first step is towards the left
From then on you cannot lose the path
You are committed to the circuit
Left brain right brain
Cross and re-cross
Always towards the centre

You can walk it on your own
At any time of day or night
Or you can take a candle
And do it in the company of friends
Surefooted in the dark
Always the questioning is different
And the path home reaches a different place
Though it is always the same

If you don't go there when you can
If you don't take the left step against the flow
The core will begin to shrink
The soft flesh will go black
And the kernel will dry up

In the centre you can see for miles
The air is sweet
And a single tree blooms straight and true
Filling the sky
With its radiant fruit.

Weird to find a labyrinth poem after my comments about the journal. Her words also make me think of our first couple therapy session last year. I didn't like it because it was like being unravelled. I couldn't sleep. I needed to be able to concentrate – it was A-level time. We kept going back and forth all the time in the hourly sessions – just like those right brain, left brain circuits. I wanted something from Tom that he couldn't understand – I'm not sure I could, even.

I know he found me too volatile and unpredictable and his instinct was to withdraw. I couldn't bear the silent treatment and pursued him, looking for the warmth I craved. This made him withdraw even more and made me even more desperate.

I get it, but it doesn't change anything. Will think about it tomorrow, as Scarlett O'Hara would say.

Found it much harder to choose the figures this time. Felt a sense of pressure to perform – be insightful, not repeat myself. Murmured something about this as I was looking at the shelves, with my back to Elinor. She said I had set out on the labyrinth, just let myself follow the path. After that I just went for it.

The strongest attraction was to the table again, with its tiny ceramic mugs, then a pine rocking chair. They were about security and went first into the basket, followed by a shiny purple glass pyramid, which was beautiful but also faintly repellent because so shiny and pointy and unnatural. A badger was next. It demanded to be chosen, though I didn't know why. There was a big round brownish pebble that also had to be included, though I didn't like it that much. The final one was a primitive mother-and-child, roughly made out of clay. That was chosen because I was sick of the shiny mother-and-child I chose last time. This one felt more real and how it is.

At first I had great difficulty knowing what to do with them all. The table and the rocking chair clearly had to take centre stage, as they had such positive vibes. They were placed firmly in the sand. I put the pyramid directly below the table, though there was no instinct to bed it down, and then the brown stone at the bottom of the tray. The mother-and-child at first was more in the middle, above the table but then had to be moved to the back of the tray. I surprised myself with the certainty in my hands. When it was done, all the attention was focused on the objects in the middle.

To get started, I had to talk my way through what I was feeling. A lot of it initially was saying I didn't know what the objects stood for. The table seemed comparatively clear and I was happy for it to stay in the middle, with the chair next to it, though the latter seemed less crucial.

The pyramid was not attractive and I wanted to move it away from the centre. It seemed to stand for the driven, analytical side of me (the work side) – and I needed to sideline it. Elinor said perhaps it had fulfilled its 'point'. That felt good and I moved it to the far right of the tray.

I stared at the sand for a time in silence: something felt wrong. I needed to bury the stone. It was too cold and too big and looked and felt dead. Things felt better after that was done, but still not right.

I kept getting stuck and Elinor kept giving me little cues. She murmured something about pyramids being burial chambers, whereas the things in the centre of the tray seemed very natural in colour and texture – ceramic and wood...

The space around the centre felt dry and empty somehow. I wanted a tree, something growing.

I felt unable to move. Not energized at all by the buried stone but couldn't move it out of the way altogether. Began to feel that the mother-and-child might hold the key. Elinor said that perhaps the mother figure was watching over the descent underground. I said I preferred her to the shiny Madonna-and-child figures on the shelves because she was darker and more real. I said she looked as if she could really shake her child.

We explored the possibility that I couldn't make the descent because of the fear of meeting her – the dark mother. I felt a stab of anxiety in my stomach.

I told Elinor about the novel I had been trying to write and my obsession with the fact that it had to be underground and the heroine had to be blind. I suddenly found it hard to breathe. Elinor asked what was underground and I said it was darkness and not being able to move.

I told her how the descent was so vital – how I had to get beyond the shiny, fake voice. That's why I hated the stone and the shiny Madonnas. She drew my attention to the badger and the fact that he lived underground. I had instinctively half-buried him to show he was underground, but he looked so friendly and light, as if waiting. Elinor said, 'It looks like you need to break open the shiny surface into the badger's world.' We explored how wide and free it was underground, with all the expanse of the runs, and I could breathe again.

I said I was also afraid that I would get to the source and it would be empty and dead. She said it was the source of all things as well as myself and was inexhaustible and precious.

We ended there, as I felt really tired and Elinor could see it.

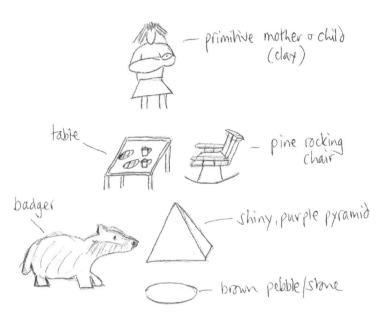

— primitive mother & child (clay)

table — pine rocking chair

badger — shiny, purple pyramid

— brown pebble/stone

What is that about the 'dark mother' who wanted to shake her child? And what is the overpowering need to break through the shiny surface and go underground, even if she is blind and scared?

Was my grandmother fiercer than I know? Are we talking about abuse? If so, why is it all coming to the surface now?

And how many of them were affected? Mother must know but she is not likely to tell me. We are good at secrets in my family.

It's mid afternoon and still sunny but the light is beginning to get more horizontal, sliding in past the hyacinth on the kitchen windowsill and lighting up the slate tiles on the floor. They are Chinese slate and full of drifts of warm colour.

Staring blindly through the kitchen window, I am aware of a growing sense of apprehension, as if the ground is shifting under me everywhere I look. Dodo is the one stable point in my life. I can't afford for her to wobble when I feel so rocky myself.

Tom was not happy when I left. The muscle in his jaw-line was twitching as he tried to prevent himself raising his voice. They don't shout in his family. I wish they would. I wish *he* would. There is so much backing up inside him. I sometimes think it would be like a furnace opening and we would all be burned to cinders, but part of me longs for the relief of it.

All the same I knew I was on sticky ground because I had made my travel plans on impulse and hadn't checked them out with him.

'You know we've got this big court case coming up. I haven't got time.'

'Mother can look after the kids.'

'Yes, but you know what Josh is like when you go away.'

'I know, but she wanted to talk to me urgently. I had to go.'

'There's the phone.'

'No. It has to be face to face.'

His features hardened. We went into lock-down. This was usually the moment when I would go into placatory mode, but this time I was not going to play.

'I've got a few days because of the college student.'

'But aren't you supposed to be working on the production together? You've only got three weeks.'

It was a good point but I couldn't concede or I was lost.

'This weekend is the only one I've got free. I'll be back by Sunday evening.'

My tone was reasonable, if not conciliatory, as I poured him a glass of his favourite Rioja. I then carried on with my preparations for the chicken and prawn paella that we all love. He turned on Radio 4, got out the Codeword in *The Independent* and we settled down to our usual, reasonably companionable routine. I think I was a bit of a shit, if I'm honest, but it seemed to work.

Josh was not so easy to deal with. He was worried about a poem they were supposed to learn for next week's English class. They never go in, whatever he does. I am beginning to suspect that he is dyslexic, but Tom is dismissive of the idea. He keeps drilling him, as if mere repetition would make it go in. It worked for him, so why not?

Jez piled in with one of her swingeing put-downs, which always reduce Josh to tears. He ran for the safety of his bedroom and I followed him, to make sure he had his bath and didn't go to bed muddy from football. We were reading some of Spike Milligan's poems together, so at least he was in a lighter mood when I told him about the trip. After a few mad poems he could almost believe that he would survive his English lesson. It breaks my heart that he is afraid of words.

Later Tom and I watched the 10 o'clock news together. After the weather, he turned the TV off and turned to face me. I don't know why he wears that shirt. It's one of those checked Viyella ones like my Dad wears. I think he believes it's reassuring for his clients. He irons them himself. I don't do ironing.

He'd obviously been giving it some more thought and had decided to try a new tack with me. His voice was very patient, but there was a bit too much indulgence in the tone.

'I know this production is important to you, but can't you

put off your trip for a week or two till work is less busy? I'm sure Dodo won't mind.'

'No, but I do.' He was using his social worker voice now, which has always irritated me. 'Dodo will be expecting me – it's all arranged.'

'I see. So her convenience is more important than mine, and the children's?'

I knew my voice was starting to rise, but couldn't hold it down: 'You know that's not it. You've never liked Dodo. That's what it's really about, isn't it.'

'Yep. I think her boundaries are shot. There's something damaged about her and it rubs off on you when you're together.'

'You don't like our closeness. That's what you don't like. We're too alike and you don't like it because you don't understand it.'

'You're wrong.' His voice had become dangerously quiet, 'I don't like it because she is trying to drive a wedge between us. This is her latest ruse to get you on your own and pour venom into your ear.'

'You're jealous! That's what it is.'

'Don't be so naive! It's obvious – you're the only one who can't see it.'

'What d'you mean?'

'Your mother, for a start. She knows what Dodo's up to. She told me only at Christmas that this has been going on all your life. Dodo has always tried to prise you away from her because she wanted a child of her own.'

'My mother wouldn't say that!'

'Well, she did. A few glasses of brandy and it's amazing what she comes out with.'

'Mother doesn't drink.'

'That's what you think. Anyway, that's not the point.'

I could see him backtracking. He knew he'd lost the moral

high ground, but I couldn't afford to fall out with him in a big way or he would make it impossible for me to get away. I said something placatory about it only taking a day or two and poured him another glass of Rioja. The waters subsided and we were able to go to bed without the duvet icing over. We even managed to give each other a kiss before turning over for sleep.

In the morning Tom dropped me off at the station on the way to work and school. Jez was quite interested in Oxford because one of the bands she likes is based there. I promised to bring her a relic. Josh was tearful but determined to tough it out, so I escaped relatively unscathed.

I didn't tell Mother the real reason for the trip of course, but as she was looking after the children I had to come up with something credible. Luckily she swallowed my excuse of consulting Dodo about the school production because she knew Dodo was in *The Winter's Tale* in her university days. I embellished it a bit by going on about the technicalities of making the statue come to life, and though I could see she was dubious, she accepted it. Thank God that she is totally ignorant of Shakespeare.

Three

3rd Meeting – 12 November

I was twenty minutes late, as I had forgotten to check the time of our appointment and assumed it was 9.30 when actually it was 9. It's usually 10am but had to be changed this time. Don't know why I keep getting the time wrong.

Felt quite flustered when I sat down in her little room. Immediately blurted out an argument with Kay yesterday. She was having a go at me as usual about how irresponsible I am. This time it was because I was going off on a trip to the Arctic to see the Northern Lights. It's for work – I'm writing an article for a Sunday colour magazine – but she resents it. I think she sees it as a waste of money – not something she could ever afford to do. But what am I supposed to do? She won't let me pay for her or the family to come too.

Found it hard to keep my cool when we were sitting there face to face and Elinor was listening so attentively. Suddenly felt that if I once started to cry I would never stop. Instead I closed the trapdoor, which I am frighteningly good at these days. We went quite quickly into the hut. It was chilly and drizzling as we walked the short distance across the garden to the welcoming hut.

I chose the primitive mother-and-child first – rough and hand-made out of clay – and put it straight into the middle of the tray. Didn't use the basket this time. Next was the ceramic table with the mugs. I was also clear that the badger had to be back as he was an important ally. I was aware of a strong need to find something to represent my inner self. It had to be refined down to a kind of kernel

– nothing shiny or false protecting it. Found a nut-like object and put it next to the mother-and-child. Also placed a green cradle opposite the mother-and-child.

Tried to let myself go with the attraction to other objects without analyzing why. Had a strong feeling today that I wanted to get to the nitty-gritty, yet also felt drawn to a tall thin goddess figure, who represented some kind of spiritual wisdom, so put them all in the sand together. The more primitive things were a tortoise and a strange creature like a long slug. The slug-like thing reminded me of some of the cave-dwelling creatures on David Attenborough's series, 'Planet Earth' the other night, who live without light and have no eyes.

Quite quickly I knew the ceramic table had to be moved out of the centre of the tray and it went to the top right. Then it was clear that the tortoise and the primitive creature had to be journeying from the table to the centre, where the nut and the cradle and the mother-and-child were, supported by the badger.

I said I thought the tortoise was probably important because of its protective carapace and Elinor said she wondered if the primitive creature was the next stage after the carapace was removed. How does she know things like that?

We explored the importance of the female goddess figure, who was very tall and elongated and seemed to be doing something ritualistic with her hands. I admitted that I didn't know who she was but I planted her in the top left-hand corner, so that she could protect and guide the mother-and-child.

The green cradle turned out to be a drinking trough on further inspection and I was clear that it could function as a trunk to carry provisions for the journey underground.

I looked a long time at the mother-and-child and said I needed to understand why it was so powerful for me and why it was so hard to look at. It was all black and purple and crudely fashioned, *like somebody who had been beaten up and put back together haphazardly. Again I had that really strong feeling that I had to stop myself from crying or I would never stop.*

Elinor didn't fill the silence with reassuring rubbish, as I would have done, but let the rope play out as far as it would go. As my gaze travelled towards the kernel/nut in the middle she commented that it looked like a seed and the seed had to go into the earth in order to flower into whatever it needed to be. She talked about the need to get right back to the original seed, to the earliest point, before all the carapaces had formed and there was the vulnerable primitive creature, with no eyes. Her words were like some deep salve applied to a wound I couldn't even name.

We left the hut and I went home. It was necessary to stop off for some coffee almost immediately, as it didn't feel safe to drive.

I am going to ring my Uncle Andy and ask him about Granny. If something went on between her and Dodo, he must know. He is several years younger than them, so would only be eleven or twelve when Dodo was sixteen, but you can't totally hide things like that. The black and blue stuff is disturbing and the power the figure has over her. Maybe that's why she went for therapy.

He is surprisingly easy to reach, almost as if he is sitting by the phone, waiting for it to ring. I can imagine him in his elegant flat in Primrose Hill, absently flicking the dust off his polished walnut bureau as he responds to orders for the expensive Persian rugs on his website.

He sounds fine until I mention that I am in Dodo's house, reading her journal and that I need to ask him something about her childhood. Suddenly the tone becomes quite agitated:

'Oh! Is Dodo there?'

'No, she has disappeared.'

'Oh! Do you think that is a good idea – to read her journal in her absence? Rather private, isn't it?'

'Yes, but she left it for me. She asked me to read it.'

'I think it would be better for you to speak to your mother first – just in case.'

'Just in case what, Uncle Andy? If there is something I ought to know about Dodo, I think it's about time you told me?'

'I'm sorry, Maggie, but I don't think it's for me to tell you.'

'Tell me what?'

'Private stuff about your mother and granny and Dodo. I really don't think it's mine to tell.'

'Did Granny ever lose her temper with Dodo? Was she ever violent?'

'Of course not! Whatever makes you suggest that? I'm sorry I have to go now. Speak to your mother.'

The receiver bangs down unceremoniously at the other end and I have an immediate image of a gilded snake sliding off into the bushes. He knows something undoubtedly but he is not going to be the one to tell.

It is nearly 5 o'clock and the sun is well and truly gone. I know it will only be a matter of time before Uncle Andy is on the phone to Mother and once she wades in the evidence will be destroyed. I put the answer-phone on, open the journal at 4th Meeting and then remember that I had better go out into the Cowley Road and get something for tea before the shops shut.

I must say she has some good shops within very easy reach. I needn't have worried – it's clear that Cowley Road never sleeps and you can get almost anything you want till about 11 at night.

My laptop is beeping, as I eat my lemon drizzle cake and finish my tea. An email from Mother is coming through thunderously:

What is this journal of Dodo's? Don't believe everything you read. Andrew has told me that you want some answers but that is not the way to get them. And why are you not answering the phone?

I shut down the lid. I don't have time for her imperative mode of communication.

4th Meeting – 12 December 2012

I arrived on time (even had time for a brief coffee in a local garden centre beforehand – execrable coffee but good for the nerves). Didn't get lost, though nearly took the wrong turning several times. Also remembered to get the money in cash.

Raised with Elinor this whole anxiety thing about being late and getting lost, as it keeps happening and I don't seem to be able to do anything about it. She said she thought that the act of driving away from the town and into the 'wild wood' was a decision to leave my capable adult self behind and move towards my child self who was afraid of getting lost. It was a step to the left towards the unconscious.

I was immediately back in my hospital bed, aged four, eyes bandaged, playing my music box as mother left the ward, not allowed to cry. For the second time with Elinor I was finding it hard to breathe. She waited. Eventually, as my breathing evened out, she said, 'What was that?'

31

I told her about my eye operation and the awful build-up to the moment when the bell went for the end of visiting each day and they had to leave. She asked how long I was in for. I told her ten days and she commented that it was about the time that Bowlby was doing his research into attachment and loss with young children in hospital.

She then asked how my mother reacted and I told her how she kept telling me to be brave and not cry and how flustered she seemed when I came out and kept clinging on to her skirt. She asked me if we had ever talked about it when I was older. I said no, it was another thing that got pushed behind the curtain and wasn't talked about.

There was silence for a bit then I told her about a dream I had had the night before, which was still hanging over me. I could only remember a bit of it but the main scene was in a hotel or conference centre where a group of us were gathered to do some task. There was a flight of shallow stairs rising from the middle of the room and the manager said suddenly that there was scuffling under the stairs which she had to investigate. She got hold of some amazing suction machine and sucked out the gap between the bottom and second stairs. A lot of rough, dishevelled, violent-looking characters erupted out of the gap. They were potentially very disruptive and frightening, but also urchin-like. I moved away, while the manager put them in a cart to dispose of them. They didn't resist.

Elinor asked me if I had any associations with the dream and I said I thought it was connected with a comment that Kay had made about me needing to beware of my fierce side when dealing with a particularly difficult colleague at work. I said it had struck home because I knew there was a ferocious side of me that was usually successfully damped down but could suddenly flare out like a flamethrower. Elinor looked straight at me (we were sitting opposite each other in her little room) and asked what it must have been like for the unacceptable and vulnerable parts of me (the urchins) to have that flamethrower directed at them.

It was quite shocking to apply it to myself and while I was assimilating the idea she added that ferocity only came about if a person or an animal was unduly restrained or mistreated, like a snarling dog constantly on a chain. It felt as if something loosened inside when she said that, but I haven't yet worked out the implications.

We went to the hut soon after and it felt very different because I knew I wanted to look at the ferocity stuff and get away from shiny shells and neat formulations. I almost felt a bit angry and dismissive and consciously looked for rougher figures. Most of the plastic fantasy figures on the top shelves seemed almost repulsive.

Really noticed, for the first time, how the more primitive and more natural objects were on the lower shelves – closer to the unconscious, I suppose, now I am beginning to get it.

As soon as we walked into the hut I felt no need to talk or follow any of the social niceties – the walk there felt like a bridge into a different world where different rules apply and there is work to be done. It's also very noticeable that I no longer feel any performance anxiety about which figures will be 'right' or look good.

I went straight to two very crude-looking animals and put them to the left of the middle, next to a rather dilapidated-looking nest that I had found on the bottom shelf. I found the tall goddess figure and put her in the top left-hand corner, half-burying her, as she seemed too ethereal but also still necessary.

In the top right corner I put a strangely repellent and sinister Asiatic figure, with a pointing finger. I think he was something to do with the flamethrower side of me. E. wondered aloud if he was repellent and sinister because he represented something I couldn't accept about myself. Maybe.

I wanted a young child to represent the disorientated figure who gets lost, but couldn't find one, so used the mother-and-child again, but said to Elinor that the baby wanted to get out of her arms. I may even have said that in a slightly irritable way, as I know I expressed *irritation about the lack of movement in all the sand trays I had made. There were never any roads, rivers or bridges, so how did I hope to get anywhere? I think I was also wanting to crack Elinor's calm detachment, but I didn't succeed. She was focused on the tray.*

After a bit she said that all the figures were turned towards the space in the middle, waiting for the event to happen. She said the nest in the middle was an empty wasps' nest, from which the stinging wasps had gone, and now it was waiting for a birth, but nothing could move yet. The baby wanted to get out of its mother's arms but couldn't yet. The primitive animals hadn't been accepted yet, so were still ugly and ungainly.

We looked at the half-buried goddess figure who had been my spiritual guide and I said I didn't want her anymore. I actually wanted to throw her to the other side of the room, but didn't say that. Elinor asked what were the good things the goddess had given me and I said permission to look at the things that matter. She asked why I no longer wanted that and I said it was time for the RECKONING. Said it in capitals and don't know where it came from. Elinor just nodded and we fell silent. Soon after that it was time to go.

goddess (half-buried)

Far Asiatic figure

primitive mother & child (reluctant baby)

primitive creatures

empty wasps' nest

I am struck by the flame-thrower and the poor urchins sucked out from under the stairs, as well as Mother's reported comment about the ferocious side of Dodo. I don't think I have ever seen her angry, though she could be sharp, particularly about careless writing. If she directed the flamethrower towards herself, maybe her absences were about depression rather than travel and adventure.

And why the stereotypical 'Asiatic' figure pointing at her in such a condemnatory way? She told me once that her granny used to threaten her with the 'yellow peril' when she misbehaved, so perhaps she is dredging that up from her unconscious. Does she know what she is guilty of? Reminds me of our couple therapy sessions, feeling weighed down by a similarly pervasive sense of guilt but not able to isolate the crime or bring it to the surface.

I also think there is some buried anger towards Elinor – some resentment of her all-knowing stance perhaps? When she says she would like to throw the goddess figure across the room, you get the feeling that she is fighting her dependence on her. I recognize that feeling.

We used to go once a week on Thursdays – after I had finished at school and before the kids got home from their after-school clubs. Tom used to work it that he was doing reports at home. I think the therapist, Judith, was probably good at her job but an hour was never long enough to let the wall down between Tom and me and besides we had to survive outside the hour.

He was always so reasonable and rational. I could see the therapist believed his story. Mine felt as if it was in a foreign language, and there was never time to translate. That image of a chained-up dog also resonates. I know I used to snarl a lot but I don't know where the rage came from.

I wasn't always angry. It's something about feeling boxed in. Tom's reasonableness makes me feel as if all my options are closed off and I am lumbering around like one of those early tanks in the First World War, unable to turn quickly enough or adapt to the new terrain.

When I look around at Dodo's house I get such a sense of space and freedom but she clearly didn't feel that. The strongest feeling I am getting so far from the journal is emptiness.

Four

5th Meeting – 9 January 2013

Seemed like a long gap since last time. Nothing burning to come out. I actually felt a bit dead and lacking in imagination. Work very pressured. Didn't take any wrong turnings or arrive late, just felt very sleepy towards the end of the drive. I suppose that is some kind of resistance too. Bright blustery day, with fierce showers now and then but long views.

When I got there we went straight into the hut as I didn't want to talk. (E. asked me which way round I wanted to do it.). Went in feeling blank and inadequate, convinced that it wouldn't work because I felt so flat.

Despite this, the figures drew me, as they always do, and there were several new ones. A red casserole dish was the first one I picked up, then a tall, thin, Masai-like figure, followed by a big squat, rather thuggish head. The next one was a primitive, snail-like figure, then a delicate, prancing, bronze horse (Greek). There was a liturgical-looking jug, which looked as if it was for pouring out libations, and finally a cradle with a baby in it. I took out the baby and left it on the shelf, as it seemed too attention-seeking or predictable to have it in.

Placed the figures in the sand in a random way round the centre of the tray, apologizing for the fact that I was finding it hard to engage, as I was still stuck in the planning, controlling mode demanded by work.

As it was, the figures did start to relate to each other in quite a dynamic way, eventually clustering round the red casserole in the middle, as if it were a centrifugal force. It seemed to represent the hearth– all that strong, red female energy. I told E. of a poem I had recently discovered about the 'red rope of love' binding mother and child. She asked me why I had left the baby out of the cradle and I said I couldn't get into all that, as I had to hold things together. Couldn't go on about my needs or the whole edifice would collapse. E. asked me if I could risk putting the baby back. I said no.

It was a day for poems and I said the squat, thuggish head represented work in the way it squatted on my life like Philip Larkin's toad, oppressing me with all its rules and regulations and deadlines. I talked about the effect it had on the beautiful horse, how it mangled and twisted it through its lack of understanding. She quite jarred me by saying that it worked both ways and the horse often dismissed the toad for being stupid and mired in mud, but that in reality they needed each other. She said the toad was also an ancient symbol for fecundity, which made me feel a lot better for some reason.

I didn't seem to be able to get away from this need to stay in the mud or go underground. We looked at the snail-like figure and I realized it should be in the bottom left of the tray, where I had been unconsciously tracing deep spirals with my hands. The libation jug also needed to be there because they were both associated with an underground temple to the Goddess I had seen in Malta, carved out of the rock, with the altar and the libation holes still there and the characteristic spiral inscriptions.

What was all this about? I knew the Masai warrior (top left) represented the increasing demands of work and the striving and perfectionism that were pulling me out too high and thin and giving me vertigo. He needed to go underground too.

At this point I told E. about last night's dream. Could only remember a fragment but in that bit I was climbing up some kind of rock face from very deep down in the earth in order to get to the session and although it was a very long way up I knew I would make it because there were good handholds right up to the surface. E. thought it was important because it showed I was not too scared to do the work with the unconscious.

After this we both fell silent and I looked at all the objects in the sand, almost as if we were looking at the contents of my unconscious mind laid out in front of us, because that was what it was, according to E. Everything I could see was part of who I was: the primitive snail, the libations jug, the squat head, the bronze horse, the Masai warrior and the cradle. After a while I went to the shelf, picked up the baby and put it back in the cradle.

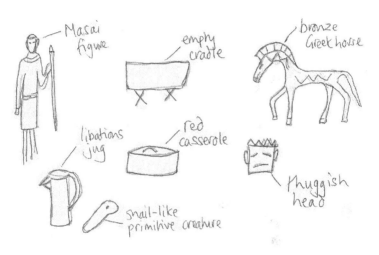

Immediately the tears began to well up inside me and I had to get outside quickly before they erupted out of my eyes and mouth like a swollen river carrying the flotsam of my life before it. I fled out of the hut and staggered blindly through the garden, trying to hold myself together. Elinor caught up with me near the house and guided me into a chair in the little room. Minutes later a cup of tea appeared. That had never happened before. She sat before me in silence for several minutes until the sobs subsided then said, 'Do you want to talk?'

When I shook my head she said, 'I don't think you should drive home for a bit. Do you know the garden centre down the road? Go and have a wander round there for a bit until you feel yourself again. Alright?'

I left and drove the couple of miles to the garden centre where I sat like a zombie for half an hour before going into the coffee shop for a second cup of tea. I was sufficiently compos mentis to avoid the coffee.

I feel quite shocked and not at all clear what finally caused the eruption. Was it the baby in the cradle or a build-up of what went before? I don't think I have ever seen Dodo cry and the thought of her so overwhelmed and fragile is very disturbing. Feels even more important to get to the bottom of this, though I feel increasingly scared as to where it's all leading.

I didn't know that she was in hospital when she was so small or that she had probably worn glasses for quite a long time before the contact lenses she acquired at university. To have your eyes bandaged and be blind and on your own in hospital for ten days at that age must have been traumatic to say the least. Is all this underground stuff something to do with getting back to that experience and somehow laying it to rest or is there something more? If she went for twenty sessions it seems likely that this was just the start. What was she trying to resolve? Something is forcing its way to the surface – that swollen river image...

There must be time for another quick look at the letters. Perhaps there is something from her time at university. I don't really know what I am looking for but that mother-and-baby image keeps coming up. Was there a baby after all? Are we perhaps talking about an abortion? Is *she* the dark mother who wants to shake her baby? Some of the ferocity she keeps referring to could be guilt.

Seems too melodramatic to be true as I look around her pristine house and see the white walls, the arty décor, the novels and poetry books, the lack of photographs. Is it a Dorian Gray scenario, with the withered portrait in the attic? It doesn't fit with the Dodo I know but maybe I saw what I wanted to see.

She was always so good with Jez and Josh – so ready to engage with their adventures, make dens with them, encourage their first attempts at drawing, Maybe that was what made Tom jealous. But when she wasn't there, those weeks and months when she absented herself, took off on her travels, I realize I don't have any idea if it was really work or something else that drove her. I can't recall any conversations where she talked about herself in any depth, or mentioned any relationships that mattered to her. I know there were several men in her life, but she never talked about them as if they were serious. Did I miss the cues? Was I so wrapped up in my own life that I didn't see?

I am constructing a whole tottering edifice out of not very much. Evidence is what we need – and quickly. I am going back to the loft.

There is a bag of photographs behind one of the boxes. Her matriculation photo from her first week at Oxford in October 1969 is on the top. She looks very stylish in her academic dress – the black mini skirt and the scholar's gown look right on her, while some of the others look uncomfortable and ungainly. She is smiling straight at the camera, as if she is exactly where she wants to be. No trauma there.

The phone rings insistently while I am up there. I have brought the handset up with me, in case it's home phoning. Surprisingly it comes up on the display with my name. I wouldn't have thought Dodo would have had it in her list of contacts, because she rarely phones. It's Tom, wanting to know when I am coming home, if Dodo isn't even there.

41

'Your mother phoned. She wants me to make sure you don't do anything silly. I have no idea what she is talking about but told her I would talk to you. She went on for about twenty minutes – something about you and a journal, but I couldn't make head nor tail of it.'

'Dodo has left me a journal to read, but she has gone away as she doesn't want to be there when I read it. For some reason Mother doesn't want me to read it and is hell bent on stopping me.'

'Why? What's so important about the journal?'

'I suspect there's a secret in it that Mother doesn't want me to know.'

'What d'you mean?'

'It describes a kind of therapy, but not the usual kind. It's in story form, so that you have to read it through to the end – all twenty chapters of it.'

'I don't get it. Why doesn't she just leave you a message like anybody else?'

'I think it was something quite difficult she was trying to say – don't yet know what it was but I am beginning to have my suspicions.'

'What kind of suspicions?'

'Well, clearly there is some kind of buried trauma and this therapy seems to have brought it to a head.'

'Was she paying for this?'

'Yes.'

'Why, if that's all it did?'

'Looks like she might have gone for some other reason – may not even have known why. Sounds like writer's block is a possibility, or even issues with work.'

'But what suspicions are you talking about?'

'Don't know really. I'm finding out so much I didn't know about her childhood. Mother never said much, but it sounds like their mother might have been a bit of a tartar. Might even have been a bit violent–'

'Whoa! Stop there! You need a lot more evidence to start throwing ideas like that around.'

'OK. I know that. I am only about a third of the way through. May even be something like a hidden abortion. There is a lot of trauma around mothers and babies, but I don't know yet if it was her as a baby or her as a grown-up.'

'And you phoned up Andrew and asked him straight out if his mother was abusive–'

'Well, it wasn't quite like that. You know Uncle Andy. He was definitely hiding something and covering for Mother, as he phoned her up straight afterwards.'

'Yes I know. She phoned me next. Just be careful. You could be stirring up a hornet's nest.'

(He is so cautious. It drives me mad. Why can't he just take my side?)

'I know, I know, but Dodo may be in trouble–'

'And that matters more than your family?'

'Of course not. Is Josh OK? And Jez?'

'They're fine, since you ask. Josh has got a friend over. Jez is holed up in her room, sulking, but I expect she'll come out for tea.'

'Oh, OK. So, we're alright then?'

'Not really. When are you coming home?'

'I've got to get to the end of the journal.'

'We need to talk.'

'We've tried that and it didn't work.'

'You didn't try! You just stuck up a brick wall and disappeared behind it.'

'There was no point in coming out – you don't hear me! We don't even speak the same language.'

'Oh, I give up! Stick with your precious journal!'

'What?'

The phone is slammed down at the other end. He is rarely that angry but I don't know what he wants from me. I can't process what is going on between us while I am focusing on the journal. It will have to wait.

My mind is all over the place. I find myself wandering round the house, picking up things randomly, looking at her treasured collection of LPs and CDs, remembering how we used to sit in those same chairs by her open fire, listening to her favourite albums, talking about politics and lovers and what we would do when we were famous. She was already famous in a small way, writing for the Sunday magazines, but she used to talk to me as if we were almost the same age.

She would sit in the blue-striped chair with the loose covers and the dodgy springs and I would curl up on the squashy sofa and we would make up stories to go with the songs. I remember particularly the ones we made up to go with 'After The Gold Rush' and 'Blackbird Singing in the Dead of Night'. They seemed to make life manageable, as if injustice and pain could be redeemed.

We rarely listened to music at home. It was a pragmatic household. We were allowed the indulgence of the *Last Night of the Proms*, the *Edinburgh Tattoo*, and Strauss Waltzes from Vienna on New Year's Day, but that was about it.

Five

The weekend with Kay in the Lake District was much on my mind, as it had left me feeling sad but also frustrated.

We talked for about half an hour in the room before going to the hut. I told Elinor about my anger and sense of manipulation but also my awareness that Kay wanted something from me at a deep level that I was not responding to. I said it reminded me of our mother who used to hoover so ferociously when we were reading the paper on a Sunday morning that she would bump the machine repeatedly into our toes. Then, as now, I wanted to shout at her, 'What is it you want from me? Just tell me straight!'

Elinor asked me what I thought was going on for Kay and I came up with some kind of resentment or envy that I had a freedom she couldn't have. I do think that's partly what's behind her behaviour, but she is so wrong. She has no idea how much I regret the path not taken. That Robert Frost poem has always done for me. I know Elinor would like to have pursued this line but it is not somewhere I want to go, so I indicated I was ready to go to the hut.

As usual I didn't know why I chose the figures – it just happened. The embracing couple, carved out of one piece of polished wood, was the first and most important object, then the hare and the bronze horse. Apart from these three, I found I wanted big objects, so I picked up a very tall king, roughly made out of clay and hand painted, and a big piece of volcanic lava.

I started with the embracing couple, putting them in the sand

45

slightly to the left of the middle. They were totally wrapped around each other and I was suddenly clear that this was what our mother had wanted from me and I had been forced to flee – for fear of being eaten up.

When I said this, Elinor asked what I meant by being eaten up. I said having my life taken over, like a ventriloquist's dummy, so that she could live hers through me. She didn't question me and I went on to put my hands on the king, who was in the top left corner, stating firmly that he was the Protector, the one who held everything together. With him there it was possible to live my own life and do the writing that I needed to do, symbolized by the volcanic rock.

I ran my hand over the rough surface of the rock, which was to the right of the couple, and commented that it needed a lot of time and concentration to heat it up to the molten state where it could be shaped. E. said that was why the king needed to be such a big figure and to have the authority of being royal. He could hold things together while I did the creative work.

I nodded, wondering who the king was, but it was nothing as simple as Dad – he was too big for that. He was almost archetypal. I said I thought I could play if he was bearing the weight. Elinor reiterated the word 'play' and seemed to think that it was very important for the writing. We agreed that I needed to find a way of protecting it when I got back home, as it kept being pushed out. I said I would mark out three regular half days in my diary. That felt good and we talked about how I could resist the guilt that came with it.

There was silence for a bit as I stroked the sand absently and wondered about the significance of the hare and the bronze horse, both of whom were grouped around the embracing couple but didn't seem to be significant this time. I wondered where Kay was in the tray, as I had come with such a sense of unease about her but I couldn't connect her with either of the figures.

Eventually Elinor murmured something about the yin and the yang and the possibility that the embracing couple could also be the two sides of me when both sides were in balance – the side I showed to the world and the inner side focused on the creative work.

Unusually for E. she was on the wrong tack. It was the original association with mother and me that was grabbing my attention. The embrace seemed to embody a sense of loss but mostly it was about the power of her grip on me and the need for something like a machete to cut her away.

Reminded me of that awful passage in the 'Northern Lights' where they sever the child from its daimon and I thought about what I had lost by allowing her to have her way. Had I killed something in myself?

Elinor went back into descriptive mode and commented that the tray seemed to be held in a kind of dynamic tension between the king, the embracing couple and the volcanic rock. I nodded and the session was over.

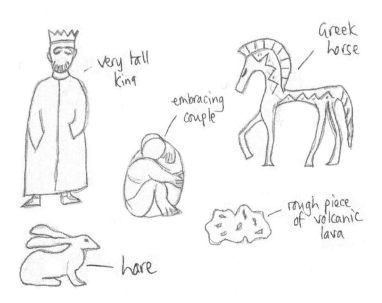

very tall king

embracing couple

Greek horse

rough piece of volcanic lava

hare

There is something new here about the crucial importance of the creative life to Dodo and how it was only possible if she cut herself off from her mother – with a machete! On the other side she seems to be saying that her mother cut her off. How can that be, if her mother wanted a closer embrace? Then there is the reference to the *Northern Lights* and the 'excision' – it looks as if Dodo is saying that something her mother did (with her agreement) was tantamount to killing her soul. What on earth is she on about?

And what has my mother to do with it all? Did she sense that Dodo was the favoured one? Was that the root of her resentment? But why would that still lead to a prickly weekend ten years after their mother had died? Something must have happened on that weekend (in January last year?) which brought it all back. What was it?

I have found her last year's calendar in the bottom drawer of the bureau, with the entry for that weekend. It says Mother and Dodo were away together visiting an old friend in Levens, an hour or so from where I was brought up. That's all I've got. I need to have a good root round to see if I can find her organizer, though I suspect she will have taken it with her wherever she has gone. It doesn't feel right to start ransacking her desk and tipping out her drawers when I can probably find the answer by reading on, but suppose something bad is happening to her and speed is vital...

The house is not very big and there aren't that many places for an organizer to be lurking. It doesn't take long to confirm that there is nothing to be found. Her laptop is here though. I can't see her saying anything personal about Kay on Twitter or Facebook, even if she uses them, but there may be something in her emails, always supposing I can guess her password.

Not surprisingly she has a Mac, so it will go straight back to where she was working, if she left it on. The battery is dead of course but the charger is here. I feel prickly with apprehension as it starts to charge up and colour returns to the screen. Will she have left me a message?

Her emails are open. There is one addressed to me, which has not yet been sent. The date is this Wednesday, two days ago, the same day she left me the voicemail. It just says, 'Please don't judge me harshly. I did it for you. The journal will explain.'

My palms are beginning to sweat, as I sit staring out of the window. It is dark now, in that dead January way when you can't believe that anything will ever grow again. Dodo only really has a yard at the back and the pots outside her window contain the skeletons of last summer's geraniums. No colour anywhere – not even early crocuses. A feeble sleety rain is starting to fall.

I really need to speak to Tom, but we're too dug into our defensive positions. What I want more than anything is for him to put his arms around me, but he doesn't do hugs.

I feel as if I have slipped my anchor and am floating away on a dark sea.

I am suddenly flooded with the recurring image I used to get when the kids were really young – about two and five. It was always an open grave, in a bleak, urban landscape, with black-suited mourners leaning over it and them trying to lower Josh's body into the hole. I couldn't let the body go and clung on to the coffin, screaming.

I still don't know what it is about. It haunted me for years and would wash over me often. Sometimes the coffin was open and he would be looking at me. It was almost a phobic fear that I would not survive if his body was wrenched away from me. I mentioned it at our therapy sessions and the counsellor became hyper alert, as if she had suddenly got a whiff of truffles, but nothing came of it. Sometimes I wonder if I am the child and it was me who was wrenched away.

I need to shake myself out of it, or I could get into panic mode. I am not used to being in an empty house, probably haven't been completely on my own for about ten years. It is 6 o'clock already and two thirds of the journal still to get through. The thought of Dodo out there in the dark and rain is not good.

I scroll idly through her emails, looking for something, without knowing what. Jude's name suddenly comes up – her old friend from school. There is a great string of emails from her, stretching back at least a year. I know I shouldn't, but I can't stop myself. The first one goes back to just before the start of the journal:

Jude, I don't know what's happening to me. It feels as if I am bleeding out. Can't work. Have had to get some help. Keep getting this scary feeling that I've become invisible and inaudible. It's as if my skin is transparent, with the blood underneath running white.

It's crept up on me in the last few months. Can hardly be bothered to eat. Everything seems so bland and tasteless – like my opinions. Not my usual self – as you know only too well!

Tried talking to a counsellor recommended by my GP, but she kept asking me how I was feeling and that's the whole point – I'm NOT feeling! Sometimes I have to remind myself to breathe. Most of the hour we sat in silence, as I didn't have the energy to dredge up a comment. Felt rude but I had to stop going.

The most attractive place is my dilapidated French bed – the one Matt and I bought together in a junk shop in the Cowley Road, when he came back to me after Marrakech. I didn't really tell you at the time but I thought he was going to stay and we tried to carry on as if nothing had happened, but I couldn't do it and I couldn't tell him. He only stayed a month. Buried myself in my Anglo-Saxon translations instead. Maybe that's it: all that unprocessed waste.

(The waste remains, the waste remains and kills.) Feels as if I am silted up inside, almost to my lips.

But I've found a solution I think. They call her 'the sieve lady' because she sieves out all the crap until you are left with the important bits. Heard a couple of people talking about her at Clara's funeral (the maverick one I liked at work) and googled her. I liked the way she described what she does – no psychobabble. Sounds different. Have made our first appointment. Watch this space!

Jude's email is pretty sceptical about therapy but generally supportive – they've been friends for fifty years so I guess they have accepted their differences. There's another one from Dodo just a couple of weeks later:

I've decided to write everything down after each session. So much happens that I need to record as much of it as I can, so that I can make sense of it later. Even do some drawings, which you would kill yourself laughing at!

The therapist is called Elinor. She is tall and arty looking, with grey hair swept back and held with a tortoiseshell clip. A bit like Elinor Bron, ironically, but more reserved and not quite so mad-looking. I go to her house near Stow-on-the-Wold and get lost on a regular basis, which is quite weird, considering how often I go.

I don't know what you would think about the process. It's certainly not scientific, but it's incredibly powerful. Reminds me of granny and her poultices – drawing the infection to the surface, so that it can't fester! All sorts of things come to the surface, though they don't necessarily get talked about.

One of the things it's brought up is Marco, the art dealer in Sansepulcro, perhaps because the novel I'm struggling with is based in his bit of Tuscany, and he's the inspiration for the main character. Without him, I don't think I could have got over Matt. What is it about Italians? Sex seems as straightforward as eating and drinking. Marco could switch from the Madonna del Parto to the physiology of orgasms at the same time as stirring the sauce.

Don't know why this novel is so hard to write. Maybe I'm no good at fiction. The whole process reminds me of that black 1300 I had, with the red seats and the dodgy gearbox. Do you remember how it got more and more difficult to change gear until finally it locked in first and ground to a halt about a hundred yards from your parents' house?

The more I work on it the tighter it gets and will soon be totally wedged. The problem is that it is really all about me and consequently it's refusing to come alive. Probably needs a shot of galvanism, but then it might well spring into life a poor, patched monster that nobody can love.

I wonder if Elinor feels like that about me. She is so supportive and positive but what if she really thinks it's all self-indulgence and I've made my bed so I'll just have to lie on it?

Jude's reply is non-committal about the Sandplay and Elinor but asks for more information about the state of her love life post Marco. Reading between the lines, she's quite concerned about Dodo's isolation and the general sense of her being stuck. She asks about her house in Oxford, as it's clear she has never seen it. Dodo replies a few days later:

I love my house. I've had it for most of my working life but not lived in it properly until I got this publishing job in the centre of Oxford. It's only a terraced house in East Oxford but it's full of light and in my mind it's like one of those white houses carved into the hillside overlooking the sea on Santorini. Do you remember those signs scrawled on the walls – 'To the Sunset'?

As you know, I have always been on the move, travelling, writing, waiting for my life to crystallize into something meaningful, but it hasn't happened. I thought Marco was the one for quite a long time, but it didn't work out. I don't think he ever seriously meant to leave Tuscany. His family was virtually built into the walls of the little hilltop town he lived in. I was just an exotic distraction.

Mind you, I've become quite an expert on Della Francesca as a result! I'm also known for my penetrating articles on Nordic light and its influence on the work of Ingmar Bergman! That came from another lovely man I met during the period you and I were out of touch, in the late nineties. Strangely, he was called Marcus. His name for me was Dorotea, which made me sound rather grand and aristocratic like Dorothea in 'Middlemarch' – especially in a Finland-Swedish accent.

I met him while I was doing a travel article on Lapland for one of the Sunday supplements. It was when the Finns were just beginning to realize the potential of trips to the Arctic Circle to meet Father Christmas and he was in the business of laying on skidoo expeditions in search of the reindeer herds.

He took me out with him on a two-day ice safari, strictly on a business basis of course! We sat round our camp fire and swapped stories as the vodka bottle grew lighter and the night grew darker, then retired to our tent, which was knee-deep in furs, and very snug and warm!

He was a Swedish-speaking Finn from the West Coast and had a surname that meant rowan tree. I told him that in the north of England it was good luck to plant a rowan tree by your back door, as it warded off evil spirits. He only smiled and passed me the bottle. He had a very engaging smile, but he was a wanderer, not somebody who ever wanted to be tied down, and, by then, I needed to.

Jude's reply makes some rude comments about Dodo's chronic Romanticism. She studied English too I think, so she knows all the terms. She goes on to ask what changed, why did she suddenly want to put down roots. Dodo's reply is oblique.

I remember when we were kids going to a concert with Dad, listening to the Halle Orchestra play 'The Flying Dutchman' and thinking there was no worse fate than being condemned to sail around the world forever without ever being allowed to land.

Banishment always seemed the worst punishment in Shakespeare too and if you weren't banished you were shipwrecked or lost in some way or another. Of his bones were coral made and all that. That's why the house is so important and why I have to stop running.

Now I am getting close to retirement, I find myself obsessively wondering if I made the right choice. Has it all been worth it? It was fine in those early years when my career was new and exciting but now everything feels so empty and pointless and it can only get worse when I retire. That's why I am doing this Sandplay thing. I am quite scared by how hard it is to get up in the morning.

Find myself thinking a lot about Mum and Dad these days, wondering what Mum would have to say about my life and the choice I made. Did I achieve what she wanted for me? Was all that education a good thing in the end? Doesn't amount to much when you lay it out end to end: an early collection of poetry, two travel books and a failed novel.

I certainly can't write anymore – except my bread and butter travel articles, which are quite formulaic – and airports have lost their allure. So here I am, 'learning to inhabit the square foot on which one stands', as Monica Furlong once put it. I am hoping Elinor will help me with that.

I walk a lot in Christ Church meadow and along the towpath down by the river. I suspect that anybody following me would have to elbow their way through air thick as porridge, populated by all the ghosts I carry with me.

And there has been no epiphany. I haven't even managed to see the Northern lights, though I have been to Lapland and Svalbard (in the wake of Joanna Lumley) several times.

Sorry for the long rant. What about you? You haven't told me how things have been since you split up with Rob.

There's a long email in response, in which Jude talks about her recent break-up. It's clear that they were both at school with her husband Rob – at least in the Sixth Form – and that Dodo knew there were problems.

She adds her reflections on men in general and Rob in particular. It appears he met up with one of his old university friends on Facebook. Jude was never on Facebook and so he was able to conduct his affair unnoticed – until one of their mutual friends alerted her. They had two children, so the fall-out was massive.

There are several exchanges about the duplicity of men but I am worried that it is getting late and I need to get on.

The emails show a side of Dodo I have never seen. To my knowledge she never mentioned either Marco or Marcus by name, but then she never mentioned Matt either – at least not to me.

Her travels and her adventures with men make my life choices seem dull and safe. Even her kitchen has an exotic, spicy smell. I can smell it now and it takes me straight back to childhood, when we used to concoct 'potions' together, mixing all the spices and sauces we could find on her shelves. If I really concentrate I can make out that the main spice is cumin, with perhaps a hint of cinnamon, and possibly cardamom. I have tried to recreate the smells and tastes in my cooking, with lots of middle-eastern recipes, but it's not the same.

Where is she and what is she trying to tell me? I'm getting really scared.

Six

We talked about the weekend in the Lakes with Kay, as I needed to understand why she had been so hostile. It was really hard going and we spent about fifty minutes in the room first – more than we have ever done. It was on my mind because things have not been right between us since and we have had several difficult phone conversations, which I want to get to the bottom of.

During the weekend Kay rubbished a travel book I had recently written and had had published and did so with a level of venom that really hurt me. There had been something wrong all weekend but she was doing her usual light, meaningless conversation until something got to her and the venom was spat out.

She took the book apart page by page with a precise and forensic contempt that left me feeling as if I had been stabbed over and over – like the shower scene in 'Psycho'. Her main argument with it seemed to be that it was superficial and not worth all the hype and the intensity of emotion was out of all proportion. I was completely incapable of answering – not least because she then ordered lunch (we were sitting in an Italian restaurant in Keswick) as if nothing had happened.

When I had finished my account, Elinor said that something in the emotional power of the story felt very primal and brought to mind the fairy tale of Snow White and the Wicked Queen, where the driving force was the queen's envy of Snow White's beauty. She asked me what kind of beauty I thought I had that Kay might envy.

Her question disturbed me but I knew straightaway what the answer was: I was always the favoured one, the princess who was given all the gifts by the good fairies at her christening. I said I thought The Sleeping Beauty was the key fairy tale and the Bad Fairy's revenge was inevitable because she wasn't asked to the party.

'So, what party was Kay not asked to?' Elinor said. I replied that our mother saw me as the one who was going to fulfil all her intellectual ambitions and Kay probably felt this. I said I thought that on the Lakes weekend it was something to do with Meg telling me first that she had been offered a new job. Kay's face had changed markedly when I mentioned it and her voice had developed an edge. Telling Elinor this, I realized that Kay would have reacted to the pleasure, maybe even triumph in my voice. Elinor waited for me to clock this but didn't comment.

I led the way into the hut, suspecting we were in for a bumpy ride. The figures almost jumped into the basket of their own accord, starting with the seal, which I laid down in the tray to the left of the middle. Unusually I was moved to put a bridge right in the centre, with a pig front left and a sharp-looking monkey front right. At the back left there was a 'House of Learning', next to a tall man in a bobble hat with binoculars held to his eyes. A sharp stick, like a spear or a dagger, was stuck in the sand at the back right.

The seal took my attention immediately as it was so ungainly and I felt I recognized my own inability to deal with the everyday problems of life in the way Kay could. I said how competent and efficient she was and that if she attacked my creative side I was left with nothing.

Elinor commented that in its own element the seal could swim with great ease and strength and I suddenly saw Kay as the seal who couldn't reach the depths and was condemned to be ungainly. It seemed clear that she needed to get over the bridge to the monkey because he had the intuition she needed, but she couldn't do it and the monkey didn't seem to have any inclination to go to her.

The man with the binoculars was playing the long game and was bolstered by the wisdom in the House of Learning but he wasn't interested in pulling it all together. The figures didn't seem able to relate to each other.

We began to concentrate on the dagger or spear that I had been resting my hand on for some time and I said that actually I wanted to stab somebody. Elinor asked me who. I was clear it was the throat of the seal and found myself jabbing at it as I tried to work out why. I was amazed by how angry I was and how much I wanted to kill it. E. said that if I cut its throat it would be mute and perhaps it had something to say first.

At one level I knew it was Kay I wanted to kill but when I tried to give the seal a voice the words that came out were about me, a slow, ungainly part of me that was small and scared and didn't want to be left behind. It was the voice of a small child being dragged along by a parent, wailing to be listened to.

I dug down and tried to find her and she was four years old and blind. I wanted to kill her because she held me back and wouldn't shut up and was often too scared to go to the places I needed to go.

After that there was nothing else to say. I felt completely drained. The Sandplay itself had taken barely half an hour and most of the figures had hardly registered. For the first time I wanted to take one of the figures with me, but I knew it was not allowed. I contented myself with cleaning the sand off the seal and requesting a Polaroid.

I drove to the garden centre very carefully and went to sleep in the car park.

It is very weird reading that my godmother wanted to kill my mother – even if only in the sand – and that something I said about my change of job had the power to set the whole thing off. I don't think of Mother as vulnerable in that way. In my eyes she has always had the power in our family and why should it matter that I told Dodo first? It wasn't a big deal anyway – I am still in the same school. I am also surprised by the strength of her reaction to Dodo's book. For Dodo to describe it as venomous, it must have been quite bad.

I can see the ungainliness, because physically Mother is a big woman – a very different genetic type from Dodo – and she is also a bit brusque, but maybe that's a red herring and the real revelation is about the ungainly side of Dodo, the part of her that drags its feet and needs attention. Maybe that needy child is the key to her disappearances over the years. Was she depressed?

Whatever was going on between the two of them was clearly a lot more powerful than I realized when I was growing up. Snow White or Sleeping Beauty? What I remember most about Snow White was how much the old Disney version frightened me when I saw it on video – all that stuff with murderous stepmothers and poisoned combs. According to Wikipedia, even the Grimms' version was sanitized and in several of the earlier versions it was the mother who was envious of her daughter's beauty. That might fit with the earlier stuff in the journal about Dodo fighting off *her* mother but I think she is right about the Sleeping Beauty being the key one for the two sisters.

Dodo seems to have been very aware of sibling rivalry between them – at least on that weekend together – and is disturbed by the venom her book excites in Mother. That's when she talks about the Bad Fairy being left out of the christening party and the curse she lays on the baby as her revenge.

I can't help feeling that Dodo's unconscious was trying to say something via this fairy story, but I don't know how it fits with what happened in the sand tray. The two sisters seem very intertwined – much more so than I have ever thought – witness the way the seal seems to stand for something they both share. It is also a strange thought that the glamorous and experienced Dodo may have in reality been the Sleeping Beauty while Mother was the one with the worldly knowledge.

Makes me see Mother's vulnerability too – possibly for the first time. I don't know why she was so disturbed by me telling Dodo about the job before I told her. Was she jealous? I do remember one Christmas when I was about thirteen, seeing Mother stare at Dodo with a look of such raw hostility that it took my breath away. We were sitting round the tree, eating mince pies and talking excitedly about the book Dodo had just given me. I remember it was *The Catcher In The Rye,* which Mother had never heard of, though we were studying it at school. I see now that she might have felt excluded, but at the time I just thought it was weird.

What fairy tale would fit my situation? *Bluebeard* springs to mind, but I know I am being melodramatic – Tom has never threatened me and anyway I have been immunized by the Angela Carter version.

Maybe the emails can elucidate some of the stuff on fairy tales. There is a bit here:

We have been talking about the Sleeping Beauty in the Sandplay sessions. Would my friends say that they can't get close to me? I think of myself as warm and easy-going. Is that wrong? Perhaps in reality I am deep-frozen.

There was something in Marcus, and in the extremes of the Finnish landscape, that exerted a terrible pull over me, so maybe that's right. But it was fire as well as ice. Marcus was both. He was the most passionate man I was ever with but you couldn't possess him. He would dictate when we met up and for how long and even when we were 'together' he used to go off on his own for days at a time into the forest or out onto the ice, when the sea was frozen in the Bay of Bothnia.

It was restful until it began to hurt but it suited me for a long time – several years. I could always find some excuse for a travel book or an article in those days – things were much more relaxed when I was freelancing.

Jude points out in a pragmatic, rather mocking tone that she writes about Marcus in a highly dramatic way so that it feels as if he is part of some kind of Nordic saga. She doesn't quite believe in him. I have to agree with her. Methinks the lady doth protest too much.

Back to the journal and the other Dodo. Is this the real one? Or is it the one I have known all my life, who is different again?

Seven

8th Meeting – 27 February 2013

Been leafing through the 8th Meeting and can't see anything crucial. There's a lot about baby seals and witches with pointy hats but the main thing seems to be Dodo's confession that she lost her cool at work. This is followed by her acknowledgement of the witchy side of herself, which she used to blame on PMT and can't anymore. I am struck by this paragraph:

It was very clear that the bear was in opposition to the baby seal and didn't give a damn about being nice to him. He would much rather be off on his own in the woods, not speaking to anyone. He was wild and fierce and a big powerful figure. In a similar way, the cowboy was the polar opposite of the pelican – that awful bird who feeds her young on her own blood – he didn't care for all this agonizing about responsibilities and just wanted to lie in the sun.

A big struggle seems to be playing out in the sand, with the figures in opposing pairs. Dodo doesn't say as much but it seems like she is trying to resolve an inner battle between her desire to be free and irresponsible and her instinct to protect and nurture.

The little girl is clearly a key figure and the black witch or the black mother, but what is the relationship between them? Is Dodo the black mother or is it her own mother?

I am conscious that I am looking for very direct answers from a process that works symbolically. It's a bit like expecting a poem to give you the coordinates for someone lost on a mountain.

I keep remembering that old Hitchcock film with Ingrid Bergman and Gregory Peck, the one with the amazing Dali dream sequence, where she is a psychoanalyst and he is her patient. He is on the run because he thinks he has killed somebody by pushing them over a ravine when they are out skiing, but she realizes that there is actually some trauma to do with parallel lines that makes him black out and lose his memory. She tracks it back to a childhood incident where he comes down a slide behind his younger brother and inadvertently pushes him into the path of a car. The eureka moment is when she sees his reaction to parallel lines of salt traced with a fork on a dark tablecloth.

What am I missing in Dodo's account? Something about her matriculation photo at Oxford is bugging me and I can't isolate what it is. I can see all their faces. I can remember Dodo's clothes and her expression: nothing out of order there. I know a lot of the people, as many of them were in her English group and remained friends. What is it then?

The photo is on the table but however long I scrutinize it I can't think what it is that is setting off a warning light in my head. The date is right. 1969 is the year she always talked of – the year Jan Palach set fire to himself in Wenceslas Square, the year when the Troubles in Northern Ireland really kicked off, the year of the Moon Landings, the year after the student riots in France. She was certainly in the thick of it, even got involved in a sit-in over access to student files in the Clarendon Building in Oxford.

But hold on a minute – she would be nineteen that year, which is surely too old. She got her A-levels in 1968 and didn't stay on for a please change to third year in the sixth form or go on a gap year, so where was she between Summer 1968 and October 1969? There was never any suggestion that she manned the barricades in France, so where did she go and why has no one ever spoken about it when we all know the stories so well?

The bag of photographs is crammed full of pictures of family and friends: lots of people from Dodo's school, Oxford pictures, holidays in Yorkshire and Cornwall. Mother and Dad are there, in their deckchairs, looking on while Dodo and I make sandcastles on the beach. I am about two so Dodo must be nineteen or twenty. Nothing two years earlier that I can see. There are endless pictures of me as a newborn baby, with Mother smiling somewhat smugly, but Dodo isn't in any of them, though everybody else in the family is.

Was she abroad? Nobody has ever mentioned a time abroad. Surely, if she was, there will be photos. Does she have a secret cache somewhere that isn't for public consumption? I haven't really looked – not systematically – and feel a bit reluctant to do something so intrusive. On the other hand, she invited me in; she wants me to find the answer.

No luck with the photos but have discovered that the letters are arranged in a kind of chronological sequence – i.e. different periods in different bags – so it is relatively easy to isolate the school and university ones. Have found an interesting one, dated November 1968, from Jude, then at Liverpool University, asking why she hasn't taken up her place at St Hilda's. It's full of gossip about their mutual friends, so that must be why she's kept it. No reply from Dodo of course, but it does take us a step further on.

The letter has also been redirected by Granny – to somewhere in Lancaster. That's only half an hour from Penrith, so she would have been very near us. Why has no one ever mentioned it? Perhaps this was the elusive relationship. Can't be Matt surely, as he would still be travelling. If I google the address, perhaps I can get an idea of who lived there – from the electoral register or something.

Have now tried that and it's too complicated for the time I've got – need to sign up to the various websites, pay fees etc, with no guarantee that I will recognize the name, if she is living with someone or it's a shared flat. Anyway, how likely is it that there will be someone else so soon after Matt? At least I have clarified that the address on the letter was a private house.

My hunch is that she went up to Lancaster to be near Mother and had an abortion or even a baby from Matt or someone else and then went off to Oxford as if nothing had happened. Have googled Mother and Baby clinics in the sixties and there is a huge amount about them – I didn't realize there was such a stigma about unmarried mothers even in the late sixties. Looks like pregnant girls had to be sent away and could only return after they'd had the baby and had it adopted. Is that what happened? There was certainly one in Preston, which is only about fifteen miles away.

Did Granny know or did Dodo do it all without telling her? She must have had help from Mother at least. Don't know who to ask. If the family haven't told me so far, they are not going to start now and the records in the homes and clinics will be confidential, so that won't help. Anyway, this could all be my fantasy and the explanation something else completely.

Tom talks to Mother. They are quite close. I think she maybe sees him as a substitute son. I know she feels that his parents neglected him, sending him to boarding school in England and not coming over from Hong Kong to visit him for years at a time. Perhaps something about Dodo and the baby might have slipped out. Do I dare phone him after our last conversation?

'Tom, I know you're angry with me but I need to ask you something–'

'Have you decided to talk at last?'

His voice has a trace of hope in it, which I know I am about to dash, rat that I am. 'If you can help me with this, I'll be able to sort this out much sooner.' I hope he can hear that I am trying to be nice.

'What do you want to know?'

He is back to his usual curt tone and my heart almost fails me. 'Has Mother told you anything about Dodo having an abortion? It would have been before she went to university.'

I can almost hear the cogs in his brain whirring round before he answers me but there is only an infinitesimal pause before he says: 'No, nothing about an abortion.'

'Well, what about a baby then?'

'You know there is no evidence of a baby.'

He is stonewalling. 'That is not what I asked you.'

'Your mother would never talk to me about such a personal family matter. You know how private she is.'

I do indeed, but there is something about Tom that softens her. I have seen it in her eyes more than once when she has been looking at him. And I can hear it in his voice now. He is protecting her.

'OK, I will carry on digging.'

'Be careful. You may be digging up something better left.'

Maybe, but it's too late now. I put the phone down with a cursory goodbye and pace about the living room, trying to process what I have just heard. Are Tom and Mother in cahoots?

Am I the only one who doesn't know the secret? If I'm right, why are they keeping it from me? Am I not to be trusted?

Eight

Sunny, but trees still bare and famished-looking.

Good drive over but felt a bit depressed. Mixture of things I think. Some of it was undoubtedly about this being our last session for two months but it was also something to do with my sense of alienation at the conference I went to in Exeter last weekend. It was all about the latest online developments in publishing, and I should have been energized, as most other people were, but it just left me cold, as if all the old certainties were slipping away and I was left stranded on some deserted shore – Matthew Arnold's melancholy, long, withdrawing roar.

I was also angry with myself for going to the conference just because Anna would have been there on her own, when really I wanted to work on the novel. It hadn't helped that some kind of festival was being celebrated and the streets were full of families.

We sat in the little room for quite a while, as I think Elinor could feel the weight of my mood and wanted to free things up a bit before we went into the hut. She probed a bit about the sense of alienation and whether it was about focusing on other people's work and neglecting my own. I came clean and admitted that I was scared of the writing and would do almost anything to avoid doing it, in case I got down to the coal seam and found it was exhausted. If it was all worked out or had never really been any good then I had nothing left and it had all been for nothing. My whole life.

I showed her a poem I had written on the way home from the conference. Might as well include it here, for the record:

Finding A Voice

Before I start to speak
I will have to find my voice
It is buried deep
At the bottom of the cupboard
Beneath the embroidered tablecloths
Left me by my granny
Beneath the box of family photographs
Tiny faded squares
Of well-behaved children
In belted coats and lace-up shoes
Underneath the old school books
With lists of declensions
And carefully coloured maps
Beyond the battered copies of
Heidi and Nancy Drew
And Alison's Island Adventure
To Where the Wild Things are
Or were
What if I reach it at last
And the colour has gone
The pattern lost?
What if it is better left?
How will I make it back
Carrying that stillborn weight
And resume the folding
Of cloths?

Of course Elinor had logged my terror about having nothing left and told me she had, but suggested we leave that to the sand tray and see what came out of it.

We walked to the hut in silence as usual and I had the familiar sense of a weight shifting down my body – away from my chest to somewhere where it could be worked with. It was almost like a transfer of power to my hands – as if they knew what had to be done and were going to get on with it.

Didn't feel as drawn to individual figures as usual. There was an overwhelming need to work with the deep-water stuff, to the point of looking for things on the sea-bed.

I picked up the white seal first but the stronger pull was towards the shells and bleached-out sea creatures on the bottom shelf. I picked up a fossilized sea anemone and placed it in the middle of the tray, protected by a thin piece of driftwood on one side and a cuttlefish shell on the other. There was a small bleached skull, perhaps a mouse's, to the right of the fossilized anemone and the primitive slug-like creature from an earlier tray to the left. Bottom left was a chalky ammonite and top left was a big piece of dark volcanic rock.

The whole tray looked bleached-out except for the volcanic rock, which I knew was the writing. I looked at the tray for a while, considering it, then added a fireman, complete with breathing apparatus, which I buried in the top right-hand corner, with an extremely ugly-looking armadillo sitting on top of him, to keep him down. He was the desire to rescue people, when I should be getting on with my own stuff, and I was pleased with myself for dealing with him so resolutely.

After the fireman, I was stuck, as everything in the tray felt so dead. Even the volcanic rock had once been part of a fiery eruption but was now burnt out.

Elinor helped me out by saying that it was important to remember that all the things in the tray had once been living things and could live again if they had water. The seal would also be able to swim. She said that for her the tray looked like the beginning of things, not the end of things.

I looked at the tray to see how water could return to the parched land – short of my picking up the jug and pouring it in. Felt very grail-like, with the Fisher-King needing to be healed before the land could become fertile again. Couldn't remember what it was that healed the Fisher-King – something about Perceval asking the right question.

It felt as if the sea anemone in the middle held the key and I instinctively drew the cuttlefish and the driftwood closer to it, as it looked so dangerously open and vulnerable – like a sunflower frozen at the moment of full opening.

Elinor noted what I was doing – pulling in the boundaries to protect the anemone – and wondered aloud what vulnerable thing at the very heart of me I needed to protect and nourish. It wasn't the writing, though that was clearly affected by what I chose to do, and it wasn't the relationships with other people, because I had buried the fireman. We looked at the bleached skull, which seemed to represent how I felt about my work and my relationships with my colleagues – nothing there to sustain me.

At that point I asked about the grail legend and she told me that Percival had to ask the Fisher-King 'What ails thee?' Hm, I wish I knew.

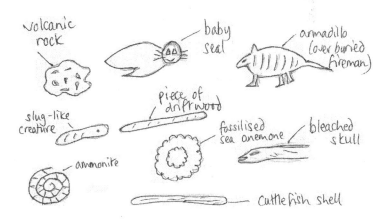

Burnt-out, bleached-out, stillborn, parched, dead – we seem to have reached a pretty desperate place. Keeps making me think of *The Waste Land* and the desperate longing for rain – 'dry sterile thunder without rain' etc. Have found the *Complete Poems and Plays* on her bookshelf and there is actually a line in Part V which has to be about the Fisher-King. I have never taught it, so am not sure, but it says: 'I sat upon the shore/Fishing, with the arid plain behind me'. It's just before that amazing line 'These fragments I have shored against my ruins'.

It is difficult to read how sad she felt seeing the streets full of families celebrating together, how excluded she felt. I always thought she was fine about coming to stay for Christmas and birthdays, but maybe it just brought home what she had lost. When I think about it, most Christmases ended with her and Mother having a row – perhaps there was more behind it than I thought.

The fossilized sea anemone seemed to carry a weight of tenderness – could that be the lost baby?

What water can resurrect a living creature turned to stone aeons ago? It's possible in plays of course – the statue of Hermione comes to life in *The Winter's Tale*. I saw it as a teenager at Stratford and thought it was a cop-out, but since then I have seen some productions that make you half-believe in the miraculous power of love and redemption. All the same, I'm probably on a hiding to nothing with the kids at school. I need to get a grip of the production before it's too late.

Sandplay is a sort of play, I suppose. It looks like you enter into some kind of trance state when it's really working. Perhaps things can be changed there, in the same way as they can in hypnotherapy.

But what is it that needs to change? What question does she have to ask and answer for herself? If there was a child, does she have to give herself permission to go and find him/her? There's a lost child in *The Winter's Tale* – Perdita – and she is miraculously recovered.

But there's a flaw to all this: we've been through nine sessions and she's never mentioned a child, a baby. Why? She can't have forgotten. Has she pushed the memory so far down that she can't recognize it for what it is? Like Gregory Peck and the fateful slide? No, he was a small child; she must have been seventeen or eighteen. Surely she can see what is forcing its way up into her consciousness. What does she think she has come to therapy for? Does she seriously think it's just writer's block? Has she thought what the block could be? A huge, baby-shaped boulder perhaps?

Takes me back to that family tree we did in couple therapy (I think they call it a genogram). We were looking at how closed-off I felt Mother was and we began to wonder if the closed-off bit in her went back to her own mother who had a child with a G.I. during the war and had to give it away to be adopted.

She never told anyone, and we only found out when we went through her private papers after both grandparents were dead. She had kept the birth certificate and it showed who he was. It all happened when her husband, my grandfather, was away on bombing missions. No wonder she was a bit of a tartar. The hole inside *her* would have been baby-shaped for sure. I can only guess how it impacted on Mother and Dodo, but it would have impacted; that much is certain.

Her poem, with its references to that wonderful book, *Where the Wild Things Are* has such powerful regret in it. She used to come and read to Josh and Jez and that was one of their favourite books. Maybe it cost her more than I thought.

I need a break. Time to put the kettle on. I think there are some biscuits somewhere.

Nine

Have gone back to the poem while my coffee is cooling. I know it's about her writing but I think something else has sneaked in – like another picture emerging from underneath when they start cleaning an old painting. Could it actually be her fear of searching for and finding her lost child – now grown up – who doesn't want to know her? 'What if it is better left?' she says and 'how will I make it back?' – to her old life, I presume. Feels extremely poignant when you read it like that, and almost desperate, but, strangely, there is no hint in the journal that she is consciously aware of it. Is she hoping I will pick up the allusion?

Either I am completely off track or she has somehow totally repressed the memory of giving birth and giving the baby away. Is that possible? Can you do that and carry on with your life as if nothing had happened? I have been in close contact with her all my life and she is a normal, sane person – funny, kind, empathetic. She has never seemed switched-off in any way. So I must be wrong – there must be another explanation.

Oddly, the newspaper I bought on the way here is open at an article about a woman who escaped from East Germany via a daring border crossing from Hungary to Austria while on 'holiday' there some months before the Wall came down. It says she 'remembered almost nothing of her flight to the West', despite the fact that she was twenty-four years old with a son of six.

She created a new life for herself in West Germany but there was hostility to the 'Ossies' (Easterners) so she did everything she could to fit in and eradicate all memories of her past life. It seems that she was so successful that she literally couldn't remember anything about the highly dangerous border crossing until she started to have flashbacks when footage of the Wall coming down appeared on TV at the twentieth anniversary. The journalist writes: 'It is almost as if the act of leaving everything behind and moving so quickly from one life to another triggered a kind of traumatic amnesia'.

Later in the article a psychologist is quoted as saying that fear, loss and shame are common among those who leave their homelands and those who survive best are those who are supported by a community of other exiles. The woman in the article did not have any such support and eventually had a kind of breakdown. She recovered by leaving her job in business and working as a gardener for six months, barely speaking to anyone. She is quoted as saying, 'That time of silence helped to bring back my equilibrium. I came face to face with reality.'

Is this a possibility? Could the Sandplay work have triggered flashbacks and led to a kind of breakdown? Maybe she can't cope with seeing anyone and has headed off to somewhere isolated. I need to read on.

10th Meeting – 15 May 2013

Very Spring-like on the drive over. Everything densely green and luxuriant. Kept thinking of George Herbert's line, 'Who would have thought my shrivelled heart/Could have recovered greenness?'

She doesn't get lost once, which she clearly regards as progress, but most of the meeting is about the new job she's applied for and how scared she feels. Doesn't advance the cause much, though there is some fascinating stuff about her and Mother:

Elinor pushed me to talk about what it was that scared me. I said it was the organizational stuff – having to keep so many plates spinning at once, the fear of missing something important, being exposed as incompetent, etc, etc. She probed a bit more and I admitted that Kay was always the organized one and I was the dizzy one, impractical and forgetful, only fit for the academic life.

'That was what your mother wanted for you, wasn't it?' she said. 'Perhaps that side of you got accentuated because it fitted the family script. Do you think Kay struggles with being the practical one rather than the clever one?'

That pulled me up short and I realized Kay and I had never really compared notes – just lobbed comments from our entrenched positions.

I had no idea that she felt so incompetent, as I have always thought of her as the independent liberated one. Never occurred to me that she would be sensitive because she wasn't like Mother. Was Mother sensitive because she wasn't like Dodo? I guess she must have been. Being an only child, I don't really understand what it's like to feel pushed out or compared unfavourably with your sister or brother.

I know Mother used to get grumpy about Dodo never being there when something practical needed doing, like getting Grandpa into a home when his Alzheimer's got bad, but I was caught up in my own ploys when the worst was happening so I didn't see most of it. Am beginning to wonder if I was a bit of a brat, but can't go into that now, as time is short.

Looking at the tray this time, it seems to be all about how she relates to her work colleagues from her lofty position in the roundhouse. As ever she seems to have trouble balancing the various bits of herself, but Elinor sorts her out by helping her reposition the firefighter so that he can be her PR person and keep her connected. She also cuts down her more grandiose claims about the roundhouse, with the result that she goes home pleased that all her mental furniture has been rearranged. Interesting, but I'm not sure it advances things much

Don't seem to be getting any closer to what she is trying to tell me and I am beginning to feel restless. Have I got time for a walk? What time is it? I am about half way through the journal and it's 7 o'clock. I've got tomorrow as well, so there has to be time for a walk round the block. It's dark but I could walk down Iffley Road to the Plain and have a look at St Hilda's, see where Dodo's room was. She told me that she had the same room all three years and you could see it from the street. Don't suppose I'll get past the Porter's Lodge but it must be freer now than it was when she was there. Worth a try anyway.

For some reason the gates are open and there is nobody in the lodge, so I am able to walk into the grounds. The whole place is lit up and a lot of smart people are gathering by the river with wine glasses in their hands. Looks like there is some event on – a concert or a talk or something. I feel very conscious of my clothes – jeans and a fleece clearly don't fit the dress code – but it's OK because I am heading for Hall Building, which is off to the right and against the flow of people.

Dodo was in a big room overlooking the street, on the second floor, next to the kitchen/pantry, which they called the Moab, after the bit in the *OT*, which says 'Moab shall be my wash-pot'. Amazing how much detail I know, when I wasn't even there. Almost as if she had to keep me up to date with every stage of her story. Odd really.

I am able to get onto the lawn on the river side of the building and see the view that Dodo always wanted but never got. She used to talk about sherry parties given by the tutors on this lawn. Seems like another age. Who drinks sherry now? Which students ever drank sherry except for Oxford types! It must have felt quite a bizarre environment after growing up in the north, so close to the gritty realities of Liverpool, still with bombed-out bits after the war.

She used to say that she longed for some beauty and couldn't wait to get away. When she went for the interview it was like visiting Eden and she couldn't believe they would let her in. I remember her showing me the telegram, which said something like, 'Will you accept vacancy?' and her laughing at the very thought of refusing her ticket out. She said there wasn't even a bookshop in the town where she lived and Broad Street (The Broad of course) in Oxford had at least three, if not four, including the magisterial Blackwells.

All the same, I know for a fact that she experienced a kind of culture shock for the first year and had to pretend she was happy because there were such expectations at home. What if there was also a lost baby? How would she cope with that amount of loss and still survive in a culturally alien environment, with academic pressure on top of everything.

You wouldn't manage to write an essay a week and have a tutorial on it, attend weekly Anglo-Saxon or Middle English seminars, go to lectures *and* fit in a social life if your life was dislocated by grief. Not even if you were desperate to extract the very last drop out of the experience. She must have either buried it very deep down (like her voice in the poem?) or my hypothesis is wrong.

Of course there is always the possibility that she was happy to give it away and get on with her life. Maybe the longing to get away was too strong. Maybe, but I don't like to think about it.

There are lights on the far side of the river: Magdalen College School playing fields, I believe. Dodo said they used to flood in the winter and sometimes even ice over. She said it was like living inside a Turner painting, with the shifting perspectives of water and sky.

I know she grew to love it but I doubt that it helped the situation at home. I think it set her at odds with her mother, even though it was the fulfillment of her dreams for her clever daughter. Although she gained so much she also suffered the usual fate of being suspended between two worlds without fully belonging to either. I know from my mother that she could be quite arrogant and dismissive too, putting them in their place in no uncertain terms, coaching them about how they should behave and speak when they came to college functions and stuff like that. No wonder there was some resentment around.

It seems so odd to think that only five per cent of sixth formers went to university then, compared with forty or fifty per cent now and people who went to Oxbridge from Northern grammar schools were almost like traitors to their class. Real people went to the new universities like Warwick or Sussex or Kent, or my own at Lancaster, universities that were radical and down-to-earth and only half-built when they were in the sixth form.

But for Dodo it was the way out and she always used to say that it gave her something that could never be taken away. I always found that a bit odd – as if everything else had been. Standing here and looking up at the building where she spent three crucial years, it is hard to believe that all that other drama was going on beneath the surface, but maybe she just chose to push it down and get on with her life. Lots of people do.

It's stopped raining and instead of turning right to go back to the house I find myself turning left over Magdalen Bridge and making my way up the High. There are still a lot of people on the street – mostly students by the look of them, looking arty and eccentric as you'd expect, so it's not hard to imagine myself back in the late sixties and early seventies, walking the streets with Dodo, sitting and discussing literature and politics in the coffee bar on the corner of Queens Lane.

She once spent her whole term's grant on a Mary Quant military-style raincoat, which she saw in a very expensive shop a couple of doors down from that same coffee bar. I expect the shop's long gone now. She kept the coat for many years and once brought it out rather sheepishly to show me.

My feet take me past the coffee bar (now a rather smart-looking tea shop) and down the side of Queen's College. I follow the high dark wall as it bends round and find myself on the threshold of a massive wooden gate, set back to my right. It's big enough to have a door in it and I have a sudden old memory of going through the door into a garden and then into a church or a chapel where there was music.

The door is slightly open now and light is streaming through. There is clearly a string quartet on there tonight: Vivaldi and Telemann. The poster identifies it as New College – this must be the back door. I am compelled to go through it and see what is beyond.

The entrance to the chapel is there but the scene immediately dislocates, as I am confronted with the displaced head of Lazarus on its bandaged stone body and I am seven years old, holding Dodo's hand, trying to make sense of this frightening apparition. There is someone else there as well, a youngish man with short blond hair, who doesn't look at all pleased to see me. Dodo is very distressed, pulling me away. We don't stop for the music, though she had promised me.

I stumble out, past all the concert-goers, and retrace my steps till I am safely back at Dodo's, breathing heavily and in desperate need of a glass of wine.

Was that him? Did she tell him about the baby?

Ten

Another session on her fear around the change of job and the even bigger fear of what she will do when she retires and there is no job to go to. There is a lot of talk about Sandplay itself in the room before they go over to the hut – perhaps she is reluctant to engage:

I asked her why she thought Sandplay was so powerful. She said she thought there was something about handling sand that took you to a different place, something about rocks and shells from aeons ago ground down to fine particles and running through your fingers. You were transported to somewhere where the unconscious was very accessible, a sort of liminal place like the line between the shore and the sea.

She said that some people didn't talk at all during the sessions and some barely used the figures, spending a lot of time just handling the sand, often in a kind of trance. Sometimes it was as if this was the only place they could play, or teach themselves to play again, and they would stroke the sand a lot, make patterns and sculptures, build mounds and bridges, use the blue base of the tray to create rivers and lakes.

I asked her if Sandplay was different with children and she said that children were completely at ease in the unconscious and barely needed an audience. The exception, she said, was children with a great deal of trauma in their backgrounds, who didn't know how to play.

When we got to the hut it took me much longer than usual to be drawn to anything. I felt fragmented and the figures felt very random – didn't connect up at all at first. I felt quite disappointed with myself for coming up with such a random collection.

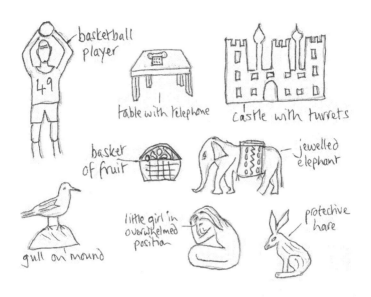

She talks about the significance of the different figures and it seems she is still struggling to balance all the admin and managerial stuff (telephone table, all-seeing gull, castle) with the need for a bit of relaxation and nourishment for herself (basketball player, jewelled elephant and basket of fruit). But then there is the little girl:

The overwhelmed little girl felt one of the most powerful figures in the tray and perhaps the source of the fragmentation – though she did have the hare next to her, as her protector.

I said I felt the little girl needed attention paid to her and Elinor agreed that nothing could move in the big world if she wouldn't put her shoes on and get dressed. That felt real and funny and reminded me so strongly of Meg when she was about three and we were trying to get her to nursery, or anywhere she wasn't ready to go to.

In terms of my own inner world, I knew she was the source of the panic and the overwhelmed feeling I often get when I can't do things. We agreed that sometimes things needed to go at her pace. I could also see that it was important she was there, because the edicts from the castle would always be more humane if they had to take account of her.

I am left with the importance of listening to the little girl who wouldn't put her shoes on.

This session hasn't touched on the central issue as far as I am concerned and I am not sure why Dodo wants me to see it, though it is lovely to have her memories of me as a little girl coming to her mind and making her smile. It doesn't feel as if this journal was written with the intention of revealing something to me. It feels as if the process forced something to the surface and she thought that I would 'get' it if she gave it to me to read. Feels like an impulsive gesture, which maybe she regretted. Could be why she bolted.

Gives me quite a pang that I never heard Mother reminisce about my childhood in the affectionate way Dodo does. It's as if her nature is too brisk for lingering over insignificant details like how long it took me to learn to tie my shoelaces. But maybe I have misrepresented her – I am beginning to wonder.

She used to teach Year 6 at my primary school, so we travelled to school together, but she would always treat me just like one of the other kids, so as not to be accused of favouritism. I understood but, all the same, I craved a bit of special attention sometimes. If she had just been capable of bending the rules occasionally it would have made all the difference, but it wasn't in her nature. She bought me books about rocks and science. I had to smuggle in real books from the library.

It was Dodo who took me to frivolous things like concerts and pantomimes, so it isn't at all odd to have that sudden memory of the two of us in New College chapel. I don't know why it hasn't come to mind before, though they do say that a certain kind of memory is anchored in place. Perhaps it's that.

Reading this last session all about Dodo's job, I wonder why Matt never appears in the sand tray. Has she 'forgotten' him so successfully that no amount of dredging will bring him to the surface? He must be a key figure in her story. Why is he not appearing?

12th Meeting – 3 July 2013

An unusually clear day, so that you could see for miles, with the Cotswold hills etched against a blue sky. Had James Taylor's 'Sweet Baby James' album on the CD player as I drove over. It was the soundtrack to my second year at St Hilda's and still has the power to bring it all back, if I don't play it too often.

Six weeks since we last met – felt like a long time. Since last time I had started the new job. Found myself saying that on balance it had been good, especially being in on strategic decisions at a high level. I admitted it had been scary – made me very aware of my weaknesses but also discovered strengths.

The new relationship with M. felt too fragile to talk about. I felt I was carrying it in my cupped hands like a Fabergé egg, terrified of dropping it.

Confessed that my unconscious ambivalence to coming here was still sabotaging my sense of direction – this time I had nearly reached the motorway going north before I realized that I had taken the wrong turning. Elinor commented that it showed the strength of my defences.

We went to the hut after about half an hour and it was so good to be back – like coming home. I felt very certain that I wanted a limited number of big solid things and they seemed to be waiting for me there. I found them very quickly and there was no need to add to them once those seven had presented themselves. At the end of the session Elinor said what a balanced tray it was and it felt like that to me – stable, dynamic and full of energy. Not always like that by any means.

I was very clear that the table with the little ceramic loaves on it was vital, as it was the secure base. I set it firmly in the centre at the back of the tray. The fossilized sea anemone went straight into the middle and seemed very unproblematic this time, as if it had earned its right to be there. Below the anemone was a big golden shell with an unfurled ear, which I knew stood for openness – allowing myself to trust and be vulnerable.

The roundhouse was there again, up in the right-hand back corner, with a big woolly mammoth very close to it. I wasn't sure this time whether the roundhouse stood for work or the writing, as it had been both before. Because the opening was turned towards the back, Elinor wondered if it stood for the creative side that had to be on hold for a bit while the world of work was dominant. That made sense to me, though it could also be while other things were dominant – more personal ones.

It was also interesting to see how the woolly mammoth gradually shifted down till it was on the same level as the anemone and could balance the power of the bird with outstretched wings in the top left corner. The mammoth was like the little girl last time. It was doing the same thing of digging in its heels and refusing to go along with things if its needs were not being taken into account. It felt very physical and not easily budged.

The seventh object was the carved embrace – carved out of one piece of hardwood – which I had rediscovered. I placed it at the left hand side of the tray, on a level with the sea anemone.

The bird and the embrace were the two that generated the greatest strength of feeling in me and there was a noticeable tension between them, almost as if they were battling for position. I felt powerfully moved by the tight embrace. It wasn't like before. Found myself weeping when I looked at it and even more when I stroked it, which I couldn't stop doing. Elinor said nothing but silently handed me the box of tissues, in time-honoured therapist fashion.

(What are you doing, Elinor? Why are you not pushing her on this? Surely you need to help her make the connection between the memory that's written in her arms and the awareness that's trying to push itself up into her consciousness like a splinter?)

The bird seemed to be saying something vital too. It was big and free and on the point of taking off. It was all about liberation and I could almost feel the weight and the power of the wings as it tried to rise into the air, but we were still tethered, something was snagging on the line.

big bird
(ready to fly)

table with
loaves & mugs

roundhouse (slightly
raised)

fossilised sea
anemone

carved
embrace

woolly
mammoth

open
shell

What is this about the bird? It feels like a breakthrough moment but it isn't clear what kind of liberation she is talking about. Maybe it's to do with the new relationship she's not telling Elinor about, the Fabergé egg.

Maybe, but there's still the embrace and the intense, tactile reaction it provoked. The stroking was almost like a primitive seeking mechanism, as instinctive as the reaction to your baby's cry when you are breast-feeding. I *know* it's significant.

Makes me think of *The Winter's Tale* again. There was an amazing RSC production I saw just a few years ago where Leontes was stroking the statue of his wife with such longing that he seemed to bring her back to life. I have never forgotten the force of those words, 'She's warm!'

Get quite tearful myself when I think about it, and also his reaction to the news that his daughter is still alive – not killed as he ordered. I always wanted to be the lost daughter that the father was so ecstatic to have returned to him.

In reality, Dad always felt distant, as if he came from another time, though he was only in his mid-twenties when I was born. He encouraged me with my schoolwork but he wasn't really very interested, because I didn't show any aptitude for maths or science. He used to look at me in a particular way, when he thought I wasn't looking, as if he couldn't believe we were related. I used to gobble up all the fairy tales where the children were changelings, in the wild hope that one day my real father would come and claim me.

Tom was probably the phantom father, if I think about it – not a mathematician of course but good at maths and interested in research and evidence, with the same cool logic. This time I could make him love me...

But nobody believes in miracles anymore, do they? Even Shakespeare has trouble pulling them off. That's why, I suppose, we're doing *The Winter's Tale* this year at school – it's the challenge of seeing if we can pull off the impossible. The kids came up with the vampire theme, which could just swing it, but I'm not holding my breath. Can you bring a vampire back from the dead or the undead? Maybe you can.

I'm going to have to sort out the staging issues and decide on whether we can adapt the text a bit. The messages are piling up on my phone and I can't ignore them much longer. I know Tom will be doing his best in my absence, so I ought to be more grateful. I heard someone say on Radio 4 the other day that it used to be staged in candlelight (before electricity I presume), which made it much easier to suspend disbelief. I'll suggest we try that.

Back to Dodo and the journal... Will the embrace start to take centre stage now or are there other places still to go? Time is moving on.

Eleven

13ᵗʰ Meeting – 10 July 2013

A horrible day for July, with rain and wind lashing the car. Despite weather I arrived on time and didn't get lost.

Couldn't find anything to talk about when we were sitting in the room and it felt quite scary, as if I were empty or as if this were the end and there was nothing else to say. Tried to explain how I was feeling, though I felt embarrassed, as if there were something wrong with me – I couldn't deliver.

Told her about a conversation I had had with a colleague at work who had rubbished the Sandplay when I had told him about it, how I wished I had never told him, but now I couldn't get it out of my mind. Made the Sandplay feel like an indulgence. The more we explored this – then and in the hut – the more I realized that it made me feel empty because I had to ignore all the struggling child-like bits of me.

Elinor helped me a lot, asking me questions about what it meant to be grown-up and helping me to see the effect of neglecting the child bits. We talked about how the child would drag at me and clamour for attention if I didn't listen to her and I was gradually able to see that it was the most important work anyone could do, at the other extreme from self- indulgence.

I told Elinor about the flat feeling I'd often had about myself as an adult, that if people got too close to me they would realize I was boring. Elinor said that the 'boring' feeling was because I was not allowing something crucial in my unconscious to express itself. The little girl was tugging my hand for the same reason.

I admitted that once, on a meditation weekend, I had had a brief sense of the flap of skin covering my unconscious being drawn back to reveal a rainforest of vivid, multi-coloured singing birds. Elinor said yes, that was what it was like when the vibrancy of the unconscious was allowed in rather than being choked off like it normally was. She talked about the amazing colour and iridescence of the creatures at the very bottom of the sea, revealed in a recent David Attenborough programme.

I was very conscious, once again, of Elinor stretching out a hand to me and pulling me up. Makes me realize what I missed when I was a child.

We went to the hut and the first thing I saw was a shiny blue/green globe, with sparkly glass drops radiating from it. It went straight into the middle of the tray, as it seemed to represent the bright singing birds.

The first figure I chose was a laid-back metal musician, playing the saxophone. He seemed to be the perfect combination of skills and creativity, someone who could be in the front and the back of his brain at the same time, in some kind of fusion. I laid him on his back middle-left.

It all seemed to be to do with the child bits of me this time. The little girl of three or four had to be included, and I had found a sturdy little figure, which I stood up in the sand very close to the sparkly globe. The primitive mother-and-baby was also there in the top right of the tray and this time the baby had to be responded to when she cried.

I talked again about the eye operation and crying in the dark without response and needing to be brave and not cry when they left the ward: the dread when I knew they were about to leave. Elinor asked what I could remember of when I came out – the fear of abandonment whenever they left me, even for a minute, in the car or in a shop.

We looked at what else had gone into the tray: the crib securely there, bottom left, with the baby in it this time, and in the middle at the top a simple, solid, wooden house. It was all about home and security.

We agreed that the baby and the small child have to come with me and I need to be patient when the paralysis/powerlessness overwhelms me – listen to them, not try to drag them along.

I don't know why I had put a fairy godmother in the top left of the tray – perhaps it was all that talk about Sleeping Beauty, but she had to be knocked over and left face down, as it was up to me to fix things. Maybe she represented Elinor and it was time to start pulling away. Perhaps it was because she was going to be away for most of August, so we would have a very long gap. She gave me a rare hug as I left, which felt very good.

Nearly 8 o'clock and I am starving. There's a menu for the local Indian takeaway on Dodo's notice-board, so that seems the obvious thing. I've ordered my usual chicken korma. Supposed to be here in twenty minutes. I suddenly feel like I used to do on an all-night essay – laying in provisions for a long siege.

That thing about feeling boring is bugging me. Makes sense that if you have suppressed a vital part of yourself what's left is kind of bland and anaemic, as if the blood has been drained out. But that's not Dodo for me, that's more like Mother. I used to wonder why she wore the clothes she did – she never wore jeans or smocks or mini skirts. In all the pictures of her teenage years (of which there are very few) she always seems to be wearing twin-sets and A-line skirts and no eye make-up. She stares out at the camera in quite a challenging way but you don't see any wild dreams in her eyes. Why?

When we used to talk about boyfriends or university or even stuff like period pains, I always got this sense of something held back, as if life was too dangerous to let go entirely. Have never really tried to analyze it before. Was she scared for me or was it something to do with her own experiences before she met Dad? She and Dad never talked about how they met, though I know it was at college. I never saw them hold hands or anything but then Mother never was one for hugs. I can only remember about two in the whole of my adult life.

Sometimes I think she must have had post-natal depression, because even in the early photos where she is holding me as a baby, she is holding me slightly at arms' length, as if I am not really a part of her. Dad never did hugs with any conviction either – he would just go off into his study and read if anything too fraught was happening. Much like Tom, if I'm honest.

Can't settle, as I'm too hungry. Keep feeling there will be other clues if only I can find them. The sitting room doesn't look like a place Dodo has staged for a final denouement. It looks like she left in a hurry, when she decided to leave me the journal. There are magazines lying around, CDs out of their sleeves, a fleece over the back of the rocking chair. She won't have had time to hide any evidence, if there is any, but what am I looking for?

Think! 'Traumatic amnesia' could be a key idea – even if it's not in the journal. The poem about finding her voice keeps coming into my mind. Not quite sure about what she means when she says 'and resume the folding of cloths' (anyone less likely to be folding cloths as a daily routine) but there is that line about the baby ('carrying that stillborn weight'), which I just assumed was her literary ambitions. Never stopped to think that her baby might have been stillborn – if there was a baby of course...

Maybe I ought to get back to Tom and ask him if the baby was stillborn. It would explain why he didn't feel the need to tell me about it, as the repercussions would have been limited. Mother might also have made him promise to keep it a secret. And if there is anyone better at secrets than Mother it's Tom – both by personality and training.

The phone is ringing out. They will have finished their tea. He is probably working on the computer in his study upstairs or finishing one of his reports and can't hear the phone.

'Yes? Tom here.'

'I think I may be going a bit mad reading this journal and imagining all kinds of things–'

'And?'

'D'you think there's a possibility Dodo could have had a baby that died, and that's why we know nothing about it?'

I am offering him a way out here, so that he doesn't have to defend his decision to keep it secret, but he's still hedging his bets.

'What makes you think that?'

'There's something in one of her poems in the journal.'

'But poems are by definition not factual accounts.'

'No, but they can reveal truths like nothing else – you know that.'

We have had this discussion many times before so we are in danger of running on well-oiled tracks. I need to take another tack.

'The journal makes it clear that there is something traumatic involving a baby and it seems unlikely that it survived, as she goes off to university so soon afterwards and there is no sign of it. It has to be either a stillbirth or an abortion/miscarriage.'

'You may well be right, but I have no knowledge of a stillbirth or a miscarriage or an abortion. I have never picked up even a whiff of such an idea.'

Why does it still feel like he is hiding something? There is almost a sense of relief in his voice. Am I asking the wrong question?

'Tom, you know from your work that Mother's generation, and the ones before, were well schooled in keeping secrets. Endless novels and memoirs about people discovering their sister was their mother and their uncle their brother – you know what I mean...'

'Maybe, but not in your family.'

'Why was Uncle Andy so secretive then and why is Mother in such a mad rush to stop me reading the journal.'

'Could be lots of reasons. Last time we spoke it was your uncle Andrew protecting you from the violence of your grandmother. Now it's something else equally far-fetched. Where is your evidence?'

He has gone back into professional mode and I can't reach him. There used to be a bridge between his kingdom and mine but we don't seem able to get across it now. He just hides away in his roundhouse, with the single window turned to the back.

'Has it occurred to you that Dodo might have given you the journal to read as a way of getting back at Kay? An act of revenge?'

'No! What for? Do you know something I don't?'

He has said too much and is backing off. 'Of course not! I just think it's strange that it's all been done with such secrecy. Anyway, that house is having a bad effect on you,' he says in a conciliatory tone. 'I knew you shouldn't have gone. Should I drive down and pick you up?'

'No thanks. Have to see it through. Will phone tomorrow.'

I can hear his sense of rebuff from here but abandoning things half way is not going to help.

A knock on the door takes my mind off it all: the takeaway has arrived.

Twelve

14th Meeting – 21 August 2013

I felt stretched out tight, lying on the surface of my life because of the pressure at work. Nothing to talk about except the demands and the struggle to hold it all together. They have advertised for a new CEO and my friendly, old-style boss is going. We have all had to re-apply for our jobs, there is no money and they are cutting out half the authors I fought for in favour of empty, formulaic stuff. Nobody with passion left.

We sat in the room for half an hour while I tried to answer Elinor's question about where I was. Surprised myself by saying I felt like one of the polar bears on the news, perching on a shrinking patch of ice in a dark sea.

E. was very patient and kept trying to feed in some reflection. Can't remember exactly what she said, which is symptomatic of how I feel at the moment.

Words didn't seem to help, so eventually we went to the hut.

Immediately I felt more real. There was sunlight pouring in through the window and sparkling on the water bucket. It was good to be back. I felt like a child, eager to play.

Hardly any hesitation about which figures I wanted. There was the old favourite of the roundhouse/tower, top right, symbolizing the inner life/creativity etc. Top left was the seagull high on a rock, representing my role at work – having to see a long way. Both of them I built up high, having wet the sand. In the bottom left-hand corner was a globe – representing head knowledge – maps, policies etc. In the bottom right was a carved wooden penguin, like the one in the 'March of the Penguins' shuffling through the frozen dark. He represented endurance, the mindless, everyday routine of putting one foot in front of the other whatever the conditions.

In the middle left was a young prince, beautiful and richly dressed, but curiously lacking in power. In the middle right was the primitive mother-and-child – vulnerable but not defensive. A big solid bridge was bang in the middle, with a round shell beneath it. Overseeing it all, in the middle at the back of the tray, was an oversize girl doll, who said, 'Don't mess with me!'

It seemed important that there were objects at the four points of a square, so that it felt secure and stable enough to do the work that was needed to integrate all the different parts. The bridge was me apparently (as were all the other figures) and my task was to connect

everything up. The tough little girl doll was there to see it all got done. The young prince was in a kind of standoff with the mother and child but it didn't look like he was going to win. I wonder if that is an omen.

The more I gazed at the figures in the sand the more my attention became drawn to the shuffling penguin, only just surviving, inching along in the Antarctic winter, protecting the egg between his frozen toes. Who was this and what was he doing there? Would he survive? I felt a huge sense of sadness about him that threatened to engulf me, as if the frozen ocean was in meltdown. I indicated I was ready to go back, not wanting a repeat of the last time.

I don't think E. noticed and we went back into the room and talked a bit about the process of Sandplay – how it is too dangerous for some people because the split-off bits of their personalities can't be contained in the box or even the hut. Sobering thought.

Feels like something is really shifting – both the mother-and-child and the penguin with the egg appearing in the same tray. Then there is also the young prince, whose power does not seem a match for the mother-and-child. She questions whether it is an omen, which must, surely, reflect her uncertainties about Matt. It is all beginning to come to a head.

Is this what happened to Dodo at the end of the Sandplay, shocking her into sharing the secret with me? Why else would she leave me the journal? I don't believe it was done as an act of revenge. I think she wanted me to discover the secret for myself by going through the same process as she had done. Why else send me all the workings as well as the solution? There are much quicker ways of revealing a secret.

I wonder if there is anything in the emails that refers to a baby. The penguin shuffling along with the egg between his toes is such a powerful image.

There's one here, following on from the ice and fire bit about Marcus:

Ice around the heart? Does that describe me? If it does, the ice is melting and feeling is starting to come back. It's like pins and needles. My dreams are full of fragments of memory, cutting into me like shards of glass. Sometimes I am holding her. I can smell her sweet baby smell and don't want to wake up. More often I am stuck in some kind of awful replay where they are pulling her away from me, out of my arms, and I am full of emptiness.

OK, so now we know. There *was* a baby. Clearly Jude knew about it, as she is not surprised, and equally clearly Dodo has not forgotten about it, has not repressed the memory, so what is happening in the Sandplay?

What is pushing its way to the surface with such force, if it is not the existence of a baby? She refers to a promise somewhere – is it the impossibility of keeping her promise anymore, her promise about the baby? Perhaps the prospect of retirement is making her question such a fundamental decision.

The phone startles me with its shrill tone. Tom's voice brings me back to earth. He sounds like he does when I am interrupting his concentration.

'Hello! It's me again. Your students have been on the phone–'

'What? Sorry, I'm a bit distracted by something in the journal.'

'Forget the wretched journal for a minute! Your students want an answer – they're saying it doesn't work.'

'What doesn't?'

'The statue bit – bringing it back to life. They say it just looks stupid. Like one of those human statues with the white faces in Covent Garden–'

'No, it does work. I've seen it work. And it's so touching when he realizes she's alive.'

'But that was the RSC, wasn't it? We're doing it in the school hall, with a load of teenagers. Are you sure you've chosen the right play?'

'Yes! The play is non-negotiable. We've got to make it work!'

'Right! Sorry I spoke.'

'What do they want me to do?'

'I don't know. Something about the vampire idea not working unless they do a massive re-write of the text, which you said they couldn't do–'

'No, they can't mess with the words, but tell them they mustn't give up. If they keep at it, it will click at some point and they'll see how to do it. Enough of them have lost a parent and longed for them to come back–'

'Do we have to have her standing on the stage all that time? It's a disaster waiting to happen. How about projecting it onto the backdrop?'

'Don't know, don't know. You might try doing it by candlelight. Can we talk about it next week? Not much time.'

'OK, if you like. I'll stall them, but it won't work much longer.'

Thirteen

15th Meeting – 4 September 2013

Feels like an Indian summer. Still warm. No sign of the leaves turning.

Felt ashamed, guilty, boring – sitting there talking about the same old issues and not doing anything about them. Why did I feel so paralysed? Why was I still so afraid of being thought a failure, incompetent and stupid?

We talked a bit about what it was like when Kay had gone away to college and there was just me. Dad was usually home late because of his job and I got the full force of Mum's attention. I explained how she had a part-time job but she was too bright for the menial office tasks she had to do and somehow not confident enough to break out and find something else, despite her time in the WAAF. Like a lot of women, I suppose, she had been pushed back into domestic life after the War and got stuck.

I said it was clear that she wasn't going to let the same thing happen to me. She was so keen to ensure that I did my homework she almost did it for me. I had no social life until after my GCEs and then only briefly because A-levels were looming.

I told E. a bit about my first boyfriend, how when I brought him home at fifteen he was almost eaten alive. They reckoned he had no ambition because he was training to be a cabinet-maker and he was too 'common' because he didn't know how to use his knife and fork 'properly'.

Matt was different. I explained how I never introduced him to Mum, but kept him separate in London, only seeing him when I went down to visit my godmother, who worked in the costume department of Covent Garden. I admitted he was the love of my life but didn't elaborate. We went straight to the hut.

When I saw the figures I had laid out in the sand I realized that they were all female, except the panther, who was at the front of the tray in the middle. At the back left was the tree with its radiant fruit. On the same line at the back, but in the middle, was a seated older woman, who looked a bit arty and was clearly an ally. At the back right, in the corner, was a robust wifey figure. She was facing down the black witch with the pointed hat, who was standing centre right. They seemed equally matched and neutralized each other like opposing nuclear deterrents. Because of that, the beautiful wispy nest in the middle (the wasps' nest again) was able to survive. A little girl was sitting next to the nest, unprotected, in the centre left of the tray. The panther was prowling in front of them.

There was a power in the tray – like an electric charge or something. I found myself stroking the panther quite a lot but I was mostly struck by how precarious the little girl was and how exposed. I could see she was only OK because of the wifey figure protecting her, but who or what was the wifey figure and who was the black witch?

I seemed to stand there for ages, in a kind of trance, searching some inner repository of unconscious images before I could come up with any answers. It was like watching an internal slideshow, clicking through the images until one suddenly leapt into focus.

The wifey was the first one to jump out at me. She was clearly Mum, and whether I liked it or not she had saved me from something black and threatening, though it had to be said that the black witch had a sleek ebony figure and a pointy head that made her irresistible to touch. She was a bit like one of those fierce Victorian ladies *dressed in mourning but festooned in sensuous jet jewellery – like Great Grandma's portrait in the family trunk. Did the little girl want to be saved? Maybe she was happy for those two to fight it out between them and leave her to get on with her life. Then there was the panther...*

She hasn't mentioned the nest. The little girl is sitting next to the nest, unprotected. What is she doing? The tree is there as well – the one from the poem, with the radiant fruit. You only get the radiant fruit if you make it to the centre, so what does it mean that it's appeared in the tray? Why doesn't she mention it?

She seems very attracted to both the witch and the panther. Does that mean she wishes she could have made off with the two of them and had another kind of life? What would that have meant for the little girl and the nest she seemed to be guarding? It doesn't feel like she wants to leave the nest, as she says it was beautiful and 'wispy', but she is clearly considering it.

It's a weird thought that you can fill a sand tray with figures from your own unconscious. I read in an article by some psychologist that we don't have one recognizable self but are all a 'community of selves', with different faces turned to different people.

But I have nearly forgotten a crucial bit: when they are talking in the room she admits that Matt was 'the love of her life' and that she used to see him illicitly in London. It can't be a coincidence that a panther has suddenly appeared in the tray? Is he still prowling around?

There must be something more about him somewhere. I need to search a bit harder. Maybe I missed something in the bag of photos or maybe there is a secret cache of letters somewhere.

There's still time and if she means me to find them they will be around somewhere. Where would I hide a batch of love letters if I wanted them to be found by the person reading the journal and no one else? I am wandering round the sitting room and the kitchen, like some kid waiting to hear 'getting warmer' and the mad thing is I am convinced that she will have found some way to let me know when I have found the hot spot.

After years of watching *Antiques Roadshow* with Tom I know where to look for secret drawers in the bureau. My heart leaps when I find one but there are no letters tied up in velvet ribbon – only a blood donor card and an old-fashioned gold ring in a box – her granny's perhaps? Mother used to talk about who got which bits of family jewellery.

I feel like a burglar as I go from room to room, rifling through the drawers and cupboards. In the bedroom, my right foot catches something sticking out from under her bed and with a lurch I realize that it is her purse – a red Tula soft leather one with dark blue trim. All her cards are there, as well as her notes and coins. It must have fallen out when she picked up her bag. She can't have gone far without any money. Surely that means that she will be back soon – wherever she is.

Her wallet has a Costa card, a Waterstones card, a Nectar card and all the usual stuff. In the Perspex bit reserved for an Oyster card or something similar is a small, black and white photograph of two very young people – a man and a woman who look like students – crammed into one of those photo booths you get at stations or supermarkets and smiling their heads off, as if they've just won the Lottery, or the Pools, or whatever it was then.

He looks a bit like Jude Law – fair and rather dishevelled with challenging eyes. She is softer, with long, dark hair parted in the middle and a 'blissed-out' look, as Dodo used to say. The woman is clearly Dodo but is this Matt? The disturbing thing is that he looks kind of familiar.

Is he still around? Surely not and yet people do find each other forty years on – Facebook makes sure of that. Could that be where she is? Is she with him? But that isn't the story the journal is telling. The journal is all about a baby – I know I am not wrong about that. So, is it his baby? Maybe he's married and there are complications. Maybe he has a family already.

Tom would say I am jumping to conclusions and need to find some real evidence, but if Matt is the big revelation, the journal will confirm it. It feels like we are really close.

There might be something in the emails too. I haven't got to the end of them. They certainly get more intense as they get closer to the present day.

Sure enough there is one dated 8th June:

Yesterday I was convinced I saw Matt on one of my river walks! It can't have been, because he was only about twenty-three or twenty-four, with that poignant half-grown beauty young men have. I wanted to bury my head in his shoulder and start again, the three of us, but he jogged past me and the moment was lost.

What have I done with my life? I am about to retire and all I can think of is the road not taken. Can't see Kay without wanting to prick her bubble. She has it all, so why does she have to rubbish my books? I can rubbish them quite competently myself. Does she see what's coming? Can't hold it in much longer. Blood will out, and all that.

Jude replies within the hour, remonstrating with her and asking if she thinks it's a good idea to dig all that up again. Has she thought of the pain it will bring?

Dodo responds in an uncharacteristic burst of pain and rage:

There's no way I can keep my promise anymore! It's like they cut out my heart all those years ago and something else has been pumping away for forty-odd years, something mechanical that's winding down like a clockwork toy. If they cut me open any time now, all they would discover is corroded machinery and wires that don't connect to anything.

The only way out is to come clean, I'm convinced of it, but how do you begin a conversation like that? I was very young? I thought it was for the best? Every line is a cliché and a selfish cliché at that.

So it *is* the promise that is forcing its way to the surface. At last we know. The Sandplay is doing its work as a poultice and the deed is about to be manifest – like Banquo's ghost, with its blood-boltered head.

Fourteen

The emails resume three weeks later on 1st July. Jude is again counselling caution but Dodo has something new to put into the mix:

I saw him again. This time he was the right age. He was walking a hundred yards or so ahead of me on the towpath. At first I thought I had magicked him out of the intensity of my memory, but I hadn't. It was definitely him – that walk, with the left shoulder slightly leading, making his gait uneven, immediately recognizable.

I was reluctant to call out, in case he turned round and it wasn't him, or I saw a lack of recognition, or even indifference in his eyes.

It didn't work the last time when we met at the concert. He was angry because I had waited so long to tell him of the baby's existence, so I couldn't begin to tell him the whole truth.

Besides, when I look back at the person I was then, I still thought I was enjoying my career and my life and I don't know what I thought would come out of it. Was I really ready to break my promise and insist on having her back? I don't think so. To my shame.

So I didn't run after him and force him to acknowledge me. Next time. I have a feeling that it has become his habit to walk along the towpath, like we used to. Maybe he is remembering as well.

Jude's emails are getting extremely edgy. She clearly doesn't think it's a good idea to renew contact with him. She reminds Dodo of the desolation it caused last time when he disappeared for months/years and was uncontactable. But she isn't listening. Clearly the momentum has become unstoppable:

He is here – in my house. I found him on the towpath, walking our route again. I don't think he recognized me when I accosted him, though he did when I spoke. His face is a lot thinner with the deep lines of a smoker. His hair is a faded blond, going thin on the crown but cut very short so that it looks grizzly and a bit French. He wears half glasses with thick tortoiseshell rims, down on the end of his nose and smokes the same old Camels. I still find him attractive when I look at him, but what does he see when he looks at me? Is it too late?

He is in the bathroom at the moment, putting his contact lenses in, so that he can see me better, or so he claims. I have almost given up on make-up now – just a bit of mascara and eye-liner. Probably too much kohl – a legacy of the sixties. Have to stop – I can hear the door opening.

It's two hours later and I am on my own again.

He was not very forthcoming when he sat down opposite me. His eyes were on my books and CDs. He was looking at the furniture and the pictures, scanning for clues about my life, maybe even the last forty years. I wanted him to know that I am at a crisis point in my life and I haven't got time to mess around, but I knew this would scare him away. We had to go through the pleasantries about work and families. All the time he was twisting a gold ring nervously on his wedding finger.

The conversation went something like this:

He said, 'I am getting divorced' (looking down at his hands).

I said, 'When did you meet? Do you have any children?'

My questions felt too blunt, though I was trying to ask them in a light, conversational tone. He seemed to accept they were necessary.

'We met at work – not long after I came back from travelling, in the early seventies.'

'Did you stay in Oxford?'

'Yes. I worked for Oxfam in Summertown, in the Information Department. Alison did too.'

'So you were working there when I was in my second and third years – all that time?'

'Yes. We stayed there for ten years before we moved to London.'

'I never saw you.'

'I saw you once, but you were with your friends, so I didn't approach. You looked happy.' He said this with some hesitation, as if unsure about the truth of it, or perhaps not sure if it was the right thing to say at my kitchen table.

We sat in silence. I still liked his choice of clothes – jeans and a faded blue shirt, with a crumpled cotton jacket in a deeper shade of blue. He was always lean and he has become leaner with age. His hands on the table were brown and sinewy, with long fingers. I always liked his hands because they were working hands, calloused and hard, but sensitive enough to be a musician's. I stretched out across the table and took them in my own.

Was I mad, Jude? You met him, so you know what he was like. Should I have resisted?

Jude is quite clear that she is deluding herself and should have kept well away, for all the reasons she knows full well, but their emails cross:

We are not lovers – yet – but I think we both want it. There is the same sexual tension between us as there always was. Maybe it is not too late to begin again and get it right. Maybe we can still be a family.

He prowls round the house, picking things up and putting them down, with a critical eye, marking his territory before he pounces. It all feels very familiar, but I am not the woman I was. I am used to more emotional foreplay.

Marco was very good at that. He would seduce me with food and wine, flirt with me shamelessly while he cooked his mother's favourite Tuscan dishes. When we eventually went to bed I would be warmed through, like a casserole after long simmering!

Matt is more of a predator, circling round me, intent on the kill, but likely to walk away without a backward glance. There is a cruel attraction in that, but I am not sure that I like myself for it.

He is asking me about my work, but he is losing interest in the answer, even as I am explaining. He doesn't want to know about my struggles with technology or difficult colleagues. He doesn't want to know about my wasted life.

He is fixing me with his intense blue eyes and I am drawn to him irresistibly. It will happen because we both need it to happen. After all these years we need to know.

Jude writes that Matt always reminded her of Sergeant Troy in *Far from the Madding Crowd* and she knows how that ended, but she is clearly aware that she can't stop Dodo. The next email is dated 4th of September.

He comes every few weeks. I get very little warning – just a brief email. The sex is fierce but curiously lacking in body, like red wine that is only twelve per cent alcohol. He never stays very long, so we haven't really talked. He says that he and his wife are separated but I am not convinced. Someone, or something, is yanking him back at strange times of the day and night.

I have been working up to telling him the truth but I know it will be the end if I do. He doesn't want to complicate his life and I don't think he wants to engage with me at that level. I don't think he ever did, but it is so hard to give up the fantasy.

I wonder if he has ever thought about her. He has never contacted me since that day when I took her to meet him and he couldn't get away fast enough, so I doubt it. We never refer to it.

I know he has a grown-up son, but they don't get on, so he rarely speaks about him. When he comes, he pads about the house in bare feet and boxers and it all seems so natural that it is hard to register how odd the situation is.

I know leopards don't change their spots, so there's not much point in hoping, but he is beautiful.

This one is followed by a long email from Jude in which she says the modern equivalent of it will all end in tears, and of course she is right. The next email says:

I have told him and it is over. As I suspected, he couldn't handle it, so now I am thrown back on myself. It feels as if the genie is out of the bottle and won't go back in again. Everything is gathering towards an end point. How will the family react if I bring the truth out into the open? It will be like lobbing in a hand grenade, but if I don't do it, I will be the hand grenade, exploding into a million jagged pieces.

I think Matt was in pain as much as I was, but it was clear that he could not take in such an uncomfortable piece of reality. It was like watching a snake trying to swallow a large suitcase with sharp corners. All that complicated family baggage. I could see he didn't have the energy for it. He seemed to shrink in front of my eyes, until he was like a husk.

I told him while we were walking along the towpath, as I had some mad idea that it would be easier in the open air. He had such a visceral reaction that we both had to sit down on a bench – near the bit where the towpath branches off down the avenue to the back of Christ Church.

I had never told him before who she was, or the fact that I knew where she was. I suppose that was the reason for the visceral reaction – all those decades living in ignorance.

When he recovered his breath, he just said, 'Why?'

I said, 'You didn't want to know.'

'You didn't try very hard,' he said.

'I promised. I couldn't go back on my promise.'

'But what about your promises to me?'

'You went away.'

'Yes, but I came back and you said nothing.'

'It was too late. I was halfway through my first year.'

'This place,' he said, looking round at the broad river with its moored college barges glinting in the sun, the golden outline of Christ Church and Merton, 'this place kills. It feeds you with romantic illusions so that you can't stomach ordinary food and you die slowly from the inside out. You should get out now, while you still can.'

He got up abruptly and I could see that there was nothing left between us. The lines on his face seemed more deeply etched as if he had aged several years in the space of our conversation. He walked off down the towpath without looking back, and I let him go.

How did she cope with such a blow? The next email gives me my answer:

I can't settle. The house feels so empty without Matt and I don't know where to begin. I suppose I knew it was never going to work but it was a powerful distraction. There is nowhere else to go now. It is clear what I must do.

I wander from room to room, picking up books randomly, feverishly scanning their pages, hoping that the words I need will appear in the middle of a chapter or jump out from the list of contents.

Once I tell her, the die is cast; there will not be a second chance.

Work is becoming intolerable. I can't concentrate. I went into a trance in the middle of an important meeting the other day and my boss was not pleased.

I keep seeing the shock on her face when I tell her. My best chance is finding some way to prepare her before we meet face to face. Maybe write something for her to find...

I am beginning to feel very anxious and afraid of what the journal will reveal. Am I the person she is scared of telling? She sounds so desperate. Will she have done something irrevocable?

Fifteen

Sitting in her room, I told Elinor how I had blown it the previous day at work and really lost my cool because nobody would help me with the transfer of files to my new laptop in the office, which wouldn't work whatever I did. Don't know why technology reduces me to tears so easily – I am always teetering on the edge of meltdown when I can't make things work. But then nothing else is working either, so why am I surprised?

My new young and efficient boss had told me in no uncertain terms that I had caused the problem myself by storing the files on my hard drive instead of the server we all share, with the result that they had all piled up and slowed down the computer so much that it had stopped working.

Elinor really took to this image of the remote laptop and the central server, where everything was stored and kept safe. I suppose she sees it as an image for herself and me.

What is all this crap about laptops and servers? Why is she not talking about the real stuff? All that agony in the emails... It's as if when they talk in the room the top slice of her anxieties gets discussed and the real stuff only comes out when she works in the sand. But she still has to recognize it for what it is.

I found myself talking about my thoughts about therapy and the exchange of money – both the giving and receiving of it – and how it bothered me. I told her about the sketch in a TV comedy show where the sympathetic teacher would be sitting there talking patiently to the pupil until the moment when the bell went off for the next lesson, when he would say, 'Fuck off, Jones'. E. didn't comment but she got it.

At least this feels real.

Went to the hut quite quickly after that and I found myself looking instinctively for something to represent the central 'server'. I wanted it to be connected to its pod or laptop by a kind of umbilical cord, so I put a big shell in the middle with a string of small shells connecting it to its 'pod' and lots more small shells in a wide circle round it. The circle was open at the bottom to facilitate the connection. Then I had my trusty badger there at the bottom left to help me keep the tunnel open to the server.

After a bit I realized I needed something more ancient and solid in the middle and replaced the shell with a primitive-looking fossil/ ammonite.

Despite all this solidity, I had a metal man sitting with his head in his hands at the top left, looking overwhelmed. There was also a rat – slimy and revolting to touch – at the centre right. He was the dark side of the therapeutic encounter and the relationship with the centre and he was there to say 'Fuck you' to the whole thing.

There were two basic sea creatures there to represent my sense that there was still a lot that was inchoate and unresolved – one top right above the rat and the other bottom right. The top right was the bleached sea anemone again and the bottom right was a reddish piece of crab shell. Had a positive resistance to any of the highly evolved figures on the shelves. E. said something about the pattern and how pleasing it was. I think she thought it looked as if everything was coming together. Maybe, but still nothing was moving.

We talked about the fossil ammonite in the centre and how it could keep things safe and allow the laptop or pod to let go of its burdens. I think I knew at some level that we were talking about our relationship and I needed to know that there wouldn't be a 'Fuck off, Jones' moment between us. When I expressed my hesitation about whether the rope would be able to take my weight, she was absolutely clear in her response without ever being explicit.

Back in the room, we managed to put some dates in the diary and acknowledged that we were on the last four. Felt very tired as I drove home, though it didn't seem as if we had done much..

Afternoon wrecked it all with technical problems on the laptop lasting three and a half hours.

man with head in hands

fossilised sea anemone

ammonite

slimy rat

small shells

badger

small shells

shell

reddish piece of crab shell

Still annoyingly oblique but I think we are getting to the nitty-gritty at last. The anxiety is certainly rising. The metal man with his head in his hands is very visible in the tray and there is a lot about testing Elinor before she lets herself fall through the trapdoor into the void. Not to mention the fact that we have an umbilical cord, even if we are ostensibly talking about computers, or the therapeutic relationship. I wonder how conscious it all is. Maybe not at all if you're in the middle of it. Reading the journal as an outsider, it's like watching the Tarot cards fall and seeing the Hanged Man, but maybe she herself had no sense of it. Maybe she kept the Sandplay and the emails in separate compartments.

It's 9 o'clock and I have four chapters to go. Mother is likely to come charging over some time tomorrow and I am not yet certain what it is that Dodo is trying to tell me or, more worryingly, whether she will have the courage to return. I thought the journal would be more direct and I would be able to read it like a diary. Instead we go round and round, backwards and forwards, more-or-less over the same ground. When are we going to reach the centre? Maybe it's a maze rather than a labyrinth and we will just get lost.

The emails seem like they were written by a completely different person – alert, self-aware, focused. Which version should I trust? And why not just tell me straight? Can it be that bad?

'Fuck off, Jones!' keeps repeating in my head, like some crazed automaton. Is that really what she thinks people will say when they read the journal? What I will say perhaps?

I am just about to make a coffee when the phone rings and it is Tom again. It is so good to hear his calm, reassuring voice and I am suddenly aware how much I need the security he provides. It is time for an apology – long overdue, if I'm honest.

'Tom, I am sorry–'

'I am sorry too, because–'

'No, I was convinced you were hiding something from me and I should have–'

'But that's just it. I was. I wasn't being honest with you and I should have realized what harm it would do. You of all people–'

'At least I am not going crazy! Will you tell me what you know?'

For once, we were not in an argument, but two adults trying to collaborate on a difficult task.

'I do know that Kay is very worried that Dodo is about to break her promise of forty years and the result will be carnage. That is why she is trying to stop you reading the journal and will probably turn up on your doorstep first thing tomorrow.'

'But why? Do you know what she expects the journal to reveal?'

'Not exactly, though I think you are on the right lines with the baby idea.'

'Oh! I just have this awful feeling that someone has been digging away at the foundations of my life and it's all about to collapse in on me. I need you here. Will you come?'

'Of course I'll come. I know you don't always believe it, but I *am* on your side. Just need to sort out some childcare and then I'll set off. Penrith to Oxford is only just over four hours if the traffic is light. Is that OK?'

'Yes, of course. I have been very paranoid and foolish, but I will try to sort my head out.'

'It's OK. I'm just glad to be talking again.'

17th Meeting – 16 October 2013

Autumn leaves beginning to fall. Conkers lying everywhere. Suddenly transported right back to my first week in Oxford and a melancholy tutorial on Tennyson – 'the woods decay, the woods decay and fall'.

The mood was still on me when we sat in the room. Talked a bit about work before we went to the hut, but I didn't really have the stomach for it.

Once we were inside the hut I felt as if I were in the right place and could get on with what needed to be done. The stage was set. One of the first things I was drawn to was a big, solid carving of mother, father and baby, made out of black soapstone. The figures were tightly wrapped together, carved out of one piece. I laid it in the sand at the back in the centre. In the middle of the tray I put a large orange plastic locust. In front of that, in the centre front of the tray was the old golden shell, unfurling towards me. The three of them were in a line.

The penguin was bottom left and the bronze horse, with its long-necked El Greco look, bottom right. Middle left, on a line with the locust, was a cooker. Balancing it on the right was the roundhouse. Wrapped round all of them was the old sinuous snake, with its red eye and sand still adhering to its scales. It felt very satisfying to complete the circle by putting the tail of the snake in its mouth.

E. seemed very engaged and said several times that it felt like a very dynamic tray. I felt it too. The primitive trinity felt very powerful and strong, as if it grounded the whole tray. There was something creative and integrating about it, as if it were talking about some kind of inner marriage as well as a physical one. Don't know where it came from when I felt so shattered inside. Reminded me of Virginia Woolf's essay about a writer's need to marry the masculine and feminine poles within herself in order to be creative. Does that mean I will always be alone?

The shell was in the middle at the front because it was unfurling and wanted to be open. I think it wanted to lay itself open to the locust, which was the destructive side of me, my own 'Fuck off, Jones'. Talked about the anger and contempt that was in me, how it had been there since I was at least a teenager. Talked about my horror when I was about nineteen and Mum had accused me of being arrogant, how I hated myself for it but it was still there, fuelling my need to make something of my life.

We looked at the roundhouse and how it kept appearing in the tray. Clearly it was more than just a place to retreat to for the writing. It was also a fortress protecting me from people's demands. E. asked who I was keeping out. I said my mother, but I think I knew there was more.

We didn't say much about the cooker, but I knew it was there to assert the importance of the independent life I have made.

The penguin was still shuffling along in the frozen dark, with the egg between its toes. It remained a figure of endurance – representing the opposite of the security of the roundhouse.

All of this was contained within the circle of the snake.

E. then said a startling thing, telling me that the symbol of the serpent or dragon eating its own tail was very ancient, found across all cultures and mythologies, representing wholeness and eternity and, in alchemical texts, the integration of the shadow.

It was almost disturbing to see such a well-known symbol emerging out of my unconscious and appearing in the sand in front of me. E. said it was called the Ouroboros and was of great significance when it appeared in a tray. I couldn't get her to say anymore than that, except to say that I needed to go away and think about what the tray was saying to me.

I had to stop on the way home because I suddenly found myself in the middle of a small market town I had never seen before and didn't know how I had got there. Everything felt very bleak but close to a resolution. Found a decent coffee shop and sat in a corner seat by the window, trying to straighten out my thoughts. Kept getting a fragment of a poem drifting into my mind:

'What is this face,
Less clear and clearer,
The pulse in the arm less strong and stronger,
Given or lent?'

The words felt really significant though I couldn't identify where they came from. It was like something had floated up from my unconscious but had fallen back before I had time to catch it.

Before the days of Google I once spent three months searching for the name of a poem from a fragment like that. Came to me in a dream in the end. My unconscious must have sifted through a lifetime's personal files and retrieved it from some musty corner.

These days it takes about a minute. Google says it is from T S Eliot's poem 'Marina', which was influenced by Shakespeare's (disputed) play, *Pericles, Prince of Tyre*. Apparently it's about a lost child saved from the sea and miraculously recovered after a lifetime's presumed loss from drowning. Looks like another *Winter's Tale*.

I can see her poetry bookshelf from here, with Eliot's *Complete Poems and Plays* next to an incomplete row of Penguin Shakespeares. No copy of *Pericles*. Don't imagine they studied it on her English course if it was a disputed text.

There's also a big old-fashioned *Collected Shakespeare*, given to her in 1968 – in that lost year between A-levels and university. According to the introduction, Shakespeare probably only wrote the end, but it's so like *The Winter's Tale*. There's a bit near the end, where Pericles first meets his lost daughter, and it actually says, 'are you flesh and blood, Have you a working pulse?' – Eliot must have read it. I wonder if Dodo did.

Have just read a bit and though it feels a bit sub-standard for Shakespeare it's very touching the way Pericles takes to the sea, searching for her inconsolably and refusing to speak to anyone. You can see the way Eliot picks this up and starts to speak of his own soul journey in terms of the making of a boat that will be seaworthy:

'I made this, I have forgotten

And remember.

The rigging weak and the canvas rotten

Between one June and another September.

Made this unknowing, half-conscious, unknown, my own...'

But then there's the bit where he seems to become almost inarticulate, as if overwhelmed by an encounter so longed-for that he can't describe it, except to say – 'this form, this face, this life'.

Dodo must have known this poem if she was haunted by those few lines. Did she manage to track it down? And if she did, what then?

If I were in her shoes, I would have been unable to stop myself going off in search of my lost child, wherever it took me. I would have moved heaven and earth to find her. As it is, it is really hard to stop myself from getting on the next train home and gathering Josh and Jez in my arms. Jez would be appalled, of course.

What about Tom? What would it take to make us come fully alive? I am reminded of the figures turned to stone by the Snow Queen in Narnia. It was the coming of Aslan that melted them. Perhaps that is my modern fairy tale. Not *Bluebeard* at all.

Sixteen

18th Meeting – 6 November 2013

Cloudy on the way, sunshine later. Geraniums still surviving in the big blue bowls in front of E.'s house.

I had been away for a weekend in Rome. Told E. how I had found it too masculine and monumental and had only been able to cope with it at night when the little squares and cafes were lit up. Had been pulled towards the Spanish Steps and the room where Keats died – also the English Cemetery where he was buried, with the heart-rending inscription on his grave, 'Here lies one whose life was writ on water'.

Told her how I had been feeling so alienated it was almost as if I were invisible and then this amazing dream came.

I dreamt I had a very young baby – still at the floppy stage – lying over my shoulder, very close to my neck. She had that wonderful baby smell and was snuggling into my neck like a blind animal. It was so lovely.

Then she was about four – wise and bright and so affectionate. She knew exactly how I felt and what I needed and was perceptive and humorous – the best conversationalist and friend you could wish for.

E. asked me who I thought she was and I said she was part of me. Told E. how completed she made me feel – a really warm, rich feeling. E. said it was a very important dream to have had because that lost part had made contact with me and told me what she needed. Felt accurate.

E. asked me what I was like as a little girl. I told her about the tomboyish bit, playing out on the street with the boys, my cap guns in

*their red and white leather holsters, how eager I was to go to school
and then the hospital experience, which interrupted everything. She
told me I should watch the Robertson/Bowlby film about the boy's
stay in hospital in the fifties but I should have somebody with me, as
it was so painful to watch.*

*Then or later she told me about the importance of sitting with
the little girl in the dark and then in the light, as it would have been so
scary for her to be lost in the dark, with her eyes bandaged. That was
probably where I went, she said, when I felt lost and overwhelmed.
Yes, the trapdoor opening, I said.*

It feels like there is some connection between this and my
recurring image of the open grave and them trying to wrench
Josh away from me. But don't really understand why.

*I was quite clear when we went into the hut that the carved embrace
was the centrepiece. Chose a big version of it and placed it in the
centre of the tray. Knew it was the little girl and me, in a tight
embrace. Felt very drawn to it in a tactile way. Found myself stroking
it when I was talking and wanting to hold it. There was a crucifix
at the top left of the tray, but I knew it wasn't the answer, as it was
like a short cut. Meditation was not going to make it go away. The
embrace was the answer.*

*I had placed a miniature version of Michaelangelo's Pieta from
St Peter's in Rome at the back right of the tray and I picked it up, but
it didn't touch me like the embrace did, so I laid it down again. The
hare was there again, to the left of the embrace, with the roundhouse
on the same level to the right. I know them now and expect them to
be there – they guard the creative and the free bits of me.*

*The man with his head in his hands was still there, at the top of
the tray, in the centre, and I knew who he was and why he was there.
E. seemed to know that I was talking about myself as well and looked*

straight at me as she said he would not be so overwhelmed if he could take the little girl with him. She reiterated that I should listen to the little girl, as she would know what I needed without hesitation, as children did when they came into the hut and started Sandplay. This filled me with joy.

The last object in the tray – at the front in the centre – was a big rough piece of rock, with a fossil in it that I knew stood for the feminine bedrock in me that I had forgotten and remembered (between one June and another September?). Explained that I had had a dream when I was nineteen or twenty, where I was walking in a long line of women about eight abreast, down a wide and shallow river, doing some repetitive ritual motion like sowing seeds. We were all carved out of rock and the dream at the time had reassured me of my femaleness when I was feeling very ugly and useless.

E. asked me what was going on at the time and I said it was my first year at university and I had just finished with somebody I had really loved. She asked me what had happened and I told her

man with
head in hands

Michelangelo's Pieta

crucifix

carved
embrace

roundhouse

hare

rock with
fossil inside

about Matt going off travelling. I could feel myself tensing up, as I thought this was going to be the day when it all came out and I would not be able to resist. Luckily the trail went cold, as we talked about Marrakech and the lure of the desert and E.'s own travels in that area. It is the first time I have felt her attentiveness waver. Why am I relieved?

Why is Elinor not putting two and two together here: the baby, the little girl, the embrace, the stone with the fossil in it? This is not inner child stuff – this is a *real* child. It is just like Freud insisting on hysteria in all those women, when the truth was that they were *actually* being abused.

When you look at her comment that the rocky woman dream came in her first year at university when she was feeling 'ugly and useless', the key word for me is not 'ugly' but 'useless'. If you've just had your baby taken away from you, wouldn't you feel useless?

And then there was her description of the warm, floppy newborn baby on her shoulder, nestling into her neck. Even in a dream you couldn't make that up, if you hadn't experienced it, but Elinor insists on relating it to her inner child. Does she actually see that there is also a real, physical child?

Does Dodo want me to see that, even though she is not spelling it out? Why is she choosing this way to reveal it to me? It's almost as if she wants me to experience the truth pushing its way to the surface in this dreamlike way, just as she did. But it doesn't fit with the emails to Jude. In those she is completely conscious of the baby and the child. What does it all mean?

I need to know how much the family knew about all this. They must have been involved in the organization and the practical details. Her mother seems to have ordered the 'excision' for a start. Did my mother know about it? Uncle Andy? I need some hard evidence of where she was between the end of her A-levels and the start of university – that's Summer 1968 and Autumn 1969. Don't think there's much point looking in the loft again; if they exist, these will be precious photos, kept somewhere safe. They won't be with the others.

There's nothing in her bureau. She has got quite a lot of photos but they are all family ones. There's a copy of Granny and grandpa's wedding photo that we've got at home, with the men still in their RAF uniform and the women in severe-looking suits and mad hats. Then there are two small albums for each of their twenty-firsts. In Mother's her friends look a bit beatnicky, though some are quite stylish in Mary Quant or Biba type outfits. In Dodo's it's all cheesecloth and velvet and smocks.

There are lots of pictures of holidays with us when I was young. I think she came with us more-or-less every year. We usually went to Cornwall , though sometimes Yorkshire and even France. We used to go in our little Ford something or other, all four of us crammed in like sausages. I used to sit with Dodo in the back – there weren't any seat belts or car seats for kids back then. We used to sing along to all the Beatles songs that she loved – she knew all the words and I did too, after she had brainwashed me.

There is a really nice framed picture of her holding me at the Christening, looking like the Good Fairy about to bestow her gifts. She is looking at me very intently as if she is really telling me something important and I am laughing. I think I was about three months. I will have to get a copy. At least it proves she was around in the Spring of 1969.

Can't find any other photographs relating to 1968 but there is something wrapped up in tissue paper in the corner of the top drawer. It's a small white stone – limestone I think – oval and smooth except for some scratches on one side that look almost like runes but could be anything. It is wrapped up very carefully, as if it was very precious, but I have seen hundreds like it on the Yorkshire coast, south of Scarborough. Maybe it was just a memento of one of our seaside holidays.

The phone is ringing. I have put it permanently on answerphone but I can hear Mother's voice clear as a bell:

'Why aren't you answering the phone? I hope you aren't doing anything stupid. We'll be with you first thing, before 9. Don't do anything before we get to you. This thing needs handling carefully. Dodo may be in a fragile state. WAIT until I tell you the full story!'

Her voice manages to sound both hectoring and distraught. She is clearly itching to get hold of me and stop me doing whatever it is she is afraid of. I am sorry that she is upset but, just as it always did, her tone is making me want to do the exact opposite.

I wonder where Dad is, if he is part of the delegation descending on Oxford or whether he is hiding out in his study as usual. I suspect she will bring him, if only to add weight. What is the 'full story' she insists on telling me? Have I got it right or will she come out with something else entirely? Is she afraid that I will learn something about her?

It's 9.45 and there are two more chapters to go. If I am to find the answer and do something about it I need to get on with it, before Mother gets here, but I am scared. If I have to go and look for her, what will I find? Thank God Tom has agreed to come down.

Seventeen

Blustery day with racing clouds. Almost blown to Elinor's. No chance of getting lost.

Told her of this image that had suddenly come to the surface three days ago in my morning meditation. It had been a particularly bad day at work the day before and my boss's attitude towards me, combined with a general sense that my life was going nowhere, had left me feeling so flattened that I felt as if I was lying prone on the floor, unable to get up.

In the picture that came into my mind I was face down in the dust, with my arms spread out, almost in a cruciform shape. But then a line came into my head, 'They that wait upon the Lord shall renew their strength'. It was followed immediately by the line: 'They shall mount up with wings as eagles'. I thought it might be from the Psalms, though I later discovered it was from Isaiah.

Anyway, the thing was that when this line came into my head the image changed from a weak, half-battered small bird, lying there helpless, into an eagle, wings only partly outstretched, biding its time.

As I watched, the image developed into the eagle beginning to flex its wings and then launch itself into the air. I had the very weird sense of feeling the drag of its wings, almost hearing them creak as they began to beat the air, but the strongest feeling was exhilaration, as we began to fly high. I was the eagle and aware of my power, knowing that I could swoop down and kill or lift up and save. It was my choice.

It felt as if I was being presented with an ultimatum: I could lie there bemoaning my fate or do something about it.

Elinor said quietly that it sounded like the unconscious had delivered up a message in no uncertain terms.

I agreed but told her there was more: I had gone with a historian friend to a celebratory service at a local church they had been restoring and it was the same day as the image had emerged. The service was called a Creation Liturgy, because it was focusing on all the amazing natural symbols carved into the fabric of the building – pinecones, lotus flowers, palm trees, fossils, dragons and eagles.

I told her that one of the readings was on the symbolism of eagles. Apparently it was a symbol of the resurrection, based on the early belief that, unlike other birds, it renewed its youth and plumage by flying close to the sun and then plunging into the water. Because it would often soar until it was lost to sight, it was also said to have the ability to gaze at the sun, so becoming a symbol of Christian contemplation. All this was fascinating but the coup de grace was the quotation that followed: the very same passage from Isaiah!

Elinor said that the eagle image and the lines from Isaiah appearing in both my inner and outer worlds was a powerful example of synchronicity, which confirmed the significance of the 'event'. She looked up the eagle in her Jungian dictionary of symbols and said that it confirmed much that had been said at the church. I could see from her reaction that she was stirred by it all, as if what she had looked for was finally happening. I recalled her saying early on that the psyche had its own timing and wondered if it was paying attention to the fact that we had only contracted for twenty sessions and it was now session nineteen.

We sat in her consulting room for about forty minutes, moving on to an exploration of the origin of the flattened feeling. Elinor wanted to know what kept me face down on the floor; what was the inhibition against speaking; why was there despair of my voice ever being heard.

I found I couldn't produce anything sensible. It had all been pressed down and compacted for so long that there were no adequate words for it. The promise had become such an inhibition against speaking that the words died in my throat. All I could do was ask if we could go to the hut. Elinor led the way.

It was the quickest session we have ever had, as there was very little to say about the images – they just were. *We were out in about twenty minutes and back to the room.*

It had been clear from the outset that it had to be the eagle in the tray but I couldn't find anything suitable on the shelves for quite a long time. Then I found the razor shells and saw immediately that I could make the eagle out of the contents of the bottom shelf – the fossils and stones and bleached sea creatures.

I picked up five things rapidly and unthinkingly. At least three of them were familiar from other times but in a sense it didn't matter which ones they were. They seemed to know their places without much help from me and lay there as if they were part of my DNA. I had great difficulty talking through their significance with E., as I didn't know what it was. E. simply said that when you reached the archetypes, there was no debate – they just were.

The eagle was lying in the centre of the tray, with its head towards the back and two straight razor shells forming the body. Its head was an old gnarled shell that looked almost like a skull and the outstretched wings came out from there, made of two more razor shells on each side, first diagonal and then drooping.

At the tip of the wing on the left was a shiny curled-up shell and at the tip of the right (as I looked at it) the fossilized sea anemone. At the base of the long body was a ceramic egg, breaking open, with flowers inside. In between the egg and the shiny shell, on the left, was a white stone, with some rune-like markings on the back. In the same place on the right hand was a perfect ammonite. They were in a straight line, except for the egg, which was slightly lower.

E. seemed particularly taken with the fact that the tray was equally balanced between straight lines and curves. I think she thought this was significant because of the integration of the male and female principles, as with the yin and the yang.

She talked about the eagle and what a powerful symbol it was, particularly here in the Sandplay context, as it not only represented power and flight but also weakness and struggle because it was prostrated in the sand, imprinted on the psyche.

I found myself drawing waves in the sand as she was talking. It felt as if the whole thing had been laid out on some ancient beach and the waves were washing over it. The egg was a sign that something new was emerging and the eagle pointed like an arrow to the black soapstone mother-and-child in the middle of the back of the tray. Everything was bleached and primitive except the-mother and-child, who were locked in their vibrant, dynamic dance.

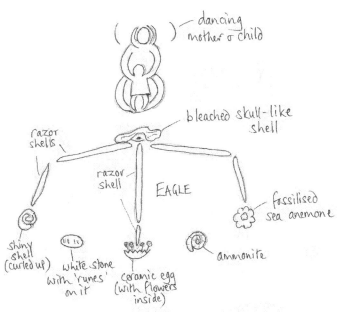

Back in the room, I said I was amazed that a Sandplay session could be so brief. E. said that when it had something to deliver, the unconscious could be very concise! She then went on to say that important things seemed to be happening in the unconscious and if I needed more time we could always extend our number of sessions. We left it open but I had a strong sense that the end was approaching and what was needed was action.

It is time to speak to Meg. Time to break my promise.

OK, we have come to the crunch point. What could be clearer? The eagle was actually pointing to the dancing mother and child!

So, if it's time to speak to me, why is she not here in person? Where is she, for God's sake? And what promise is she about to break?

This is making me very nervous. I feel like tearing up the house, emptying out all the drawers and cupboards, springing the floorboards for hidden stashes, but what am I looking for? A body?

When I was about twelve I used to have lots of dreams of corpses being buried under the compost and beginning to sprout, or walled up and bulging through the rose-patterned bedroom wallpaper or flushed down the toilet and blocking up the waste pipe. There was always that awful dream knowledge that something catastrophic and inevitable was about to happen – once we started spreading the compost, re-papering the walls, getting the plumber in.

I don't know why but in the dream it was always me who was going to be found out. Sometimes the feeling of foreboding would last into the daytime and dog me for days, but I could never talk about it. I knew that Mother would not want to hear that kind of fanciful stuff. She would have that tight, closed look that made me feel I was a disappointment to her.

I have often had the same feeling with Tom, if I wake in the night with a bad dream – particularly if I wake up crying. He doesn't want to hear about it, or he makes perfunctory soothing noises. He clearly thinks I should just get over it and go back to sleep, but I need him to hug me, particularly when it's the open grave dream and they are tearing Josh away from me. Perhaps I need to tell him. Novel thought!

There's some chocolate in the fridge. Dodo would always have some in her big bag when she came to see us, particularly if I was ill. She would bring chocolate and comics.

I feel really anxious that she has something terrible to tell me. I can feel it in my stomach – just like when I was small. Makes me want to check that Jez and Josh are alright. I always get this kind of feeling when something is going on with them, as if the umbilical cord is still attached and is stretched too tight. Reminds me of Dodo's image in the sand, with the server and the umbilical cord.

What could be so terrible that she is scared to tell me? Mother is certainly implicated, or she wouldn't be trying so hard to stop me reading the journal.

What if it wasn't me who was afraid of being found out? What if those corpses behind the bulging wallpaper were not mine but Dodo's, or even Mother's? There is certainly something in the sand that is refusing to stay buried.

Did Mother do something to Dodo's child? Did she force her to give it away? No, that doesn't make sense, because she kept coming back to see us and there was no obvious acrimony.

Anyway, why now? It's over forty years ago. Why is it all coming to a head now? And why is it so vital to tell me? It has to be something that would alter our relationship. Do I have a secret cousin? Is she threatening to reveal all?

Clearly the therapy was necessary because something was

shifting, or becoming unbearable, yet she keeps trying to push it down, even as she is trying to pull it out and look at it. I don't get it.

I imagine the twentieth session makes it obvious that she can't shirk it anymore, but it looks like it's bad enough for her to bolt and not confront it head on.

I still haven't accounted for that missing year, but I think I know what I would find, if the evidence were available.

Time to put the kettle on and find a biscuit. It's 10pm and I need some sustenance before the final push, as my grandfather would say.

It's not raining or snowing as I look out the back, so I put my jacket on and take my coffee out under the stars. It's a very clear night and consequently freezing. The air is almost ringing with cold. The silver birch near her back door is luminous in the moonlight. A young rowan tree leans towards it.

I try and bring her face to mind. It keeps shifting, with different images from the past merging and separating, so that it is hard to keep a stable picture. I have a sense of her perfume permeating the garden, though it can't be. What do they call that – an olfactory hallucination?

I have an almost physical sense of her very near and coming closer, as she waits for me to read the final pages. (*More distant than stars and nearer than the eye).*

I'd better get on with it – the Valkyries can't be far away. I wouldn't put it past them to ride through the night!

Eighteen

20th Meeting – 18 December 2013

Cold and bright. Sense of Christmas in the air. Came back another way.

Felt like quite a short session in the room, as if we both knew that we had reached the right place and there was no need to discuss it further. Before we went into the hut for the last time, E. said that she wanted to give me something to symbolize the place I had got to, as she realized that I might need strength for what I had to do. We didn't discuss what that was but she handed me the white stone that had appeared in the tray last time we met.

She said that the scratches on the back were probably not runes but it had always pleased her to think that they might be. She quoted a bit from Revelation that said, 'To him who conquers I will give a white stone with a new name written on it, which no one knows except him who receives it.'

I was deeply touched. From what I have read, it is anything but normal practice. I felt as if I had been really 'seen' for the first time in my life. It was the polar opposite of the 'Fuck off, Jones' moment.

I crossed the garden for the last time, with the stone in my pocket, my fingers wrapped around it, reassured by its solid presence. The ground was hard and glittery beneath my feet.

In the hut it took me longer than usual to find what I wanted. I suppose I was unconsciously looking for something to sum it all up, but I tried to just let it emerge, as it always had.

The obvious first choice was the carved embrace, which I put in the middle. My second choice was the lighthouse, which went to the top left. Then I found myself looking for things equally big and solid. Found a great seal at the back of the animal shelf, big and wonderfully seal-like, and put it top right. The black witch, with her sceptical eye and her down-to-earth realism, sat comfortably bottom left. Finally I found a big, pitted, ancient stone and stuck it bottom right, to represent all that was still to be resolved. The whole picture was four square and satisfying with a numinous inner core and I enclosed it with the sand-encrusted snake, the Ouroboros, with its tail in its mouth.

When it was completed there was an unusual silence – almost like a great sigh – as if it was finished and there was nothing more to say. Ite, missa est. When I looked at it I saw it was a mandala, which I knew was a symbol of integration and completion.

Elinor agreed, but continued to sit in silence opposite me, watching me stroke the carved embrace, which I half-knew I was doing but couldn't seem to stop. Then she said something very unusual. She said, 'Look at what your hands have been stroking all the time we have been speaking. Look at where you have put it in the tray. Your unconscious is drawing your attention to something very important. You need to act on it.'

I felt as if I had been propelled down a slope very fast – like when I was learning to ride my first two-wheeler and my Dad gave me a sudden push down the hill–

I am jerked into the present. The doorbell is ringing. The phone is also ringing. I pick up the phone and walk towards the door. My hand is on the latch.

'Don't answer it!' Tom is saying. (How does he know? Can he hear the doorbell?)

'Kay phoned ten minutes ago to say she is minutes away.'

(He never calls her Mother.)

'The police have also just phoned to say she has had an accident and is in A & E.'

'She isn't!'

(I am opening the door as I speak.)

'She's at the door and has just forced her way in! The police are behind her though, so I will have to go and deal with them. Will phone you back.'

Mother has her mouth open like a fish, but all I can hear is the voice of the young female PC, who is speaking quietly and sympathetically – not at all as they are supposed to speak:

'Are you Margaret Frost?'

(She looks up from her notebook and I nod.)

'I am afraid there has been a serious accident on the M40. I am very sorry but it is possible your mother may not survive. You need to come with us. We have a car outside.'

'There must be some mistake. This is my mother.'

'Yes, I am her mother!'

(Mother elbows forward and glares at the PC. I want her to prevail, as she always did, but suddenly it is all falling into place.)

'I am sorry, there is no mistake. Maggie is down as next of kin.'

Everything goes black.

Nineteen

12 January 2014 (real time)

I wasn't out very long and the young policewoman took me in her patrol car. I could see 'Mother's' car in the mirror, following. The air was full of the crackle of random communications on her radio. We didn't talk beyond practicalities, for which I was grateful. I texted Tom to say I was on my way to the hospital and asked him to come as soon as he could. I didn't have the strength to explain.

My head was full of a Simon and Garfunkel song that Dodo used to play. One line kept repeating in my head:

'*He turned on the gas and he went to sleep, with the windows closed so he'd never wake up...*'

I couldn't stop it repeating. Over and over.

When we got to the hospital the PC took me straight to her – through the floppy double doors and into a private room where she lay hooked up to a million machines. 'Mother' was not in evidence, though I knew she would be soon, so I didn't have long.

What could I say? Dodo was lying there with her eyes swollen shut and her face livid and bruised as if she had been brutally assaulted. I had been on such a long journey with her that it was cruel in the extreme not to be able to share it with her, but it wasn't going to happen.

I didn't know what to call her, as 'mother' was already taken, but it seemed crucial to give her her proper title after so long without it. I tried 'Mum' quietly, hoping for some spark of recognition but there was no discernible sign that she had heard me. Perhaps there was a slight movement around the eyes, but I could not be sure.

Then the machines started to beep in a frantic way and the monitor showed her heart rate flatlining. I had seen it all too many times on ER. The crash team rushed in and applied the paddles. It all felt very brutal and I felt protective of her bruised body at the same time as praying for a miracle.

They had just given up when 'Mother' rushed in, dropping her bags as she ran. We looked at each other with a look that was too dense to quantify.

She sat down on the far side of Dodo, her sister, and stroked her hand. I held her other hand, my mother's hand, for the first and probably the last time.

'She's warm', I said, looking at the black monitor in disbelief. My aunt shook her head robustly. She was never one for fiction.

We were ushered out while the nurses removed the tubes and tried to make her look peaceful. We both sat there on the hard plastic chairs in the corridor, staring at the pale green hospital walls, unable to begin the long process of reconstruction that was ahead of us.

But of course she didn't die.

This being a miracle 'play', she came back to life, pulled back along the tunnel by the force of our desire. In truth, it would have been easier if she had died, because now we had to do the hard bit.

You would expect 'Mother' to have come off worst, to lose everything when the truth was revealed and the prodigal sister returned, but it wasn't as simple as that. Tom, for a start, proved to be Kay's greatest advocate. He argued for the sentence she had already served to be taken into consideration, for her steady commitment and care against all the odds to be weighed in the balance. For her forty years of silence and keeping of the promise.

We started our conversations after Dodo's miraculous return from the dead, while we sat by her bed, waiting for her to regain consciousness. They say that even people in a deep coma can still hear, so we quite consciously began to probe the past in her presence, believing that when she returned she would have absorbed the bits she needed to absorb.

We played some of her favourite music on a portable CD player that I brought from her house. We played her 'California on My Mind' by James Taylor, 'Oliver James' by Fleet Foxes, 'Blackbird' by the Beatles, and everything in between. We felt like the Pied Piper, luring her back by the power of our songs.

For the first time, probably in my life, Kay/Mother talked about herself and I listened, without interrupting or switching off. I realized I had misjudged her, that there was love there, as well as the pain of the knowledge of her own infertility. I realized what she had given me – something solid at the still centre of a turning world.

She was also honest enough to admit her rage and resentment against Dodo, that she had let go of something so precious, something that Kay could never have naturally, and now she was coming back to claim her rights when all the hard work was done.

It turned out that it was Dodo's decision to give me to 'Mother', that she wanted the academic dream so much that she put up very little fight when their mother suggested it as a resolution to the problem. Apparently there had been an ectopic pregnancy and too much damage to the tubes for Kay and Cliff ever to try again.

It felt even stranger to say 'Cliff' instead of 'Dad', even though I had never felt quite like his child. Was Matt my real father?

It felt too much to go there, particularly after those emails.

Dodo/Mum finally came round one night when I was sitting with her on my own. It was about three in the morning and cold. There was only a night light on by her bed, so her voice, when it emerged from the shadows, was quite a shock.

It was a fully formed sentence, like those infants who don't bother with random nouns but come out with something complete like 'please don't put shampoo in my eyes'.

She said: 'I have been a coward. I should have told you face to face, and years ago.'

'Yes,' I said.

She slid off into sleep again, but opened her eyes abruptly after forty-six minutes. My follow-up question felt urgent, so I allowed her no respite.

'Why did you choose the journal to tell me? It wasn't as if you didn't know what was struggling to come out. You talked to Jude about it in the emails.'

'I know. I wanted you to know more about me and there never seemed to be an opportunity to talk at any depth. Perhaps I was too scared to try.'

I felt a pain in my heart as I saw my part in the avoidance – my instinct to evade the intimate moments – something Tom always insisted I did but I denied.

'Why did you do the Sandplay? Did you not know what was eating away at you?'

'Maybe you can't believe it – I don't really believe it myself – but I thought I was OK with it, that it was all in the past. I had a good relationship with you. I thought it didn't make any difference that you didn't know I was your mother.' (She hesitated over the word, saying it quite cautiously, as if she felt she didn't have any right to it.)

'So, what drove you into therapy then?'

'I think it was the feeling of meaninglessness. I was scared that one day I might just not bother to get up.'

'And now? Was it worth it?' I surprised myself by the anger in my voice.

'You have every right to be angry. It's only now that I realize what I've missed.' She moved restlessly on the pillow and I regretted my anger when she was clearly so weak.

'Kay needs to hear this as much as I do. We need to get her in here tomorrow. Sleep now.' I touched her arm in farewell and went off to her house for the first unbroken sleep I had had in a week.

Next morning, I picked up the journal again from where it had become buried under letters and messages on the kitchen table. Five days had passed since I dropped it to answer the phone and the doorbell.

I went straight to the last page, to see how it ended, looking for what I had missed when I first picked it up from her table. There was the sentence about being propelled down the hill on her first bike and then the words 'It is clear I must tell her', followed by 'I will do it once Christmas is over', which is all I saw when I turned to the back of the book in my impatience for the answer.

What I had neglected to do was turn the page – probably my guilt at rushing to the denouement. If I had, I would have seen something in her best italic writing, written with the special pen she used for calligraphy. It said, 'To my daughter, Meg, with all my love, in the hope that she will understand and forgive me.'

I cried, for the first time, as I expect she knew I would, but I still thought that the journal was a strange way to tell me something so important.

Tom, when he came back to Oxford to see me this afternoon, was in total agreement. It would be fair to say that his reaction was a little more forceful than that, but he had a right to it, after all my partisan defence of Dodo's unorthodox methods of communication. I have been unfair to him and I know I have a lot of work to do to restore the trust between us.

He has been telling me about his visit to his own mother, this week. I still blush when I think of how I demolished his faltering attempts to re-establish contact with her. He doesn't regard it as a great reunion – he still refers to her tellingly as 'Lady Edith' – but it gives him some pleasure to think that she is not ashamed to be on his arm at the university gala he has booked for them both to attend.

It is all very strange. I have even thought of Sandplay for Tom and me, as a way of coming to terms with our 'mothers', because talking doesn't seem to get us far enough. It feels as if both mothers have been displaced from their proper places like dislocated collarbones and need to be pushed back in, but neither of us knows how to do it, or is brave enough to start.

We managed to mount a successful school production of *The Winter's Tale* despite everything, though I still don't think the 'miracle' quite came off. Tom was the production manager as usual and did his best with the smoke and mirrors, keeping it just this side of hysterical. Kay came for the first time in our long history of school productions and was complimentary. We are continuing our conversations, but it is hard going. I think she would prefer it if she could draw me a diagram.

I have thought about searching for Matt but I have very little heart for it. Cliff was the dad I had when I was growing up and he did his best. It would be cruel to consign all that dogged affection to the rubbish dump. And what about Jez and Josh? They love their Granny and Grandpa and are loved back – probably more robustly than I ever was. Instead, we need to figure out a new place for Dodo. That is going to be the real task.

Tom is being very gentle with me but I want him to read the journal, so that he understands what it was all about. Not sure that he will have much patience with it but it is part of my new plan to share the difficult stuff, rather than lock it away. We might even find some revealing symbols for our own reconstruction work in the continuing couple therapy.

Perhaps he is the tall king after all and not the roundhouse with its one window turned to the back. Who am I? Sometimes I am the black witch with the pointy hat and too many times lately I have sat down and screamed, refusing to put my shoes on, so there is still work to do.

Tom tells me that he and Kay have overlapped quite a lot while they have been taking turns looking after the kids and being there for me. They both enjoy cooking, so they have spent quite a lot of time together. On one of these occasions, Kay apparently asked him if he had seen the journal and if it made any sense. He told her he had only looked at it briefly, but he knew where it was if she wanted to see it, as I had left it behind for the first time only that morning en route to the hospital.

'Show me!' she had said with her characteristic brusqueness.

He had pulled it out from under the pile of junk mail on the table and pushed it over to her, watching her expression closely as she examined it.

'I don't understand,' she had said impatiently after a few minutes, pointing to the page of drawings where the eagle was laid out in razor shells and a skull. 'What are these?'

Tom said he had agreed that it didn't make sense out of context, but he thought, from what I had told him, that the eagle appeared in the sand tray when it became clear that Dodo needed to tell me the truth.

'Why?' was her immediate response.

'Because the eagle was ready to fly,' he had told her.

'But why was that significant?' she had persisted. 'I don't understand.'

'No, I don't really either,' he had conceded, 'but I think it's about visualization – when we can see our way forward and believe in a course of action then we have the strength to do it.'

Clearly this hadn't cut the mustard. 'But why did she take more than forty years to tell her?'

'I think you have to ask Dodo that,' he had finally replied.

Grunting to herself, she had taken the teapot over to the sink to empty it, swirling the tea leaves round (she had brought her own) with an impatient jerk. 'I am too old for all this,' she had said wearily. 'Why could she not have just let it lie?'

Several months on, I think we all have more of a handle on it now. I suspect that each of us in our own way has been in survival mode for more years than we knew, sensing that the ground was unstable beneath us but not understanding why. Kay understood immediately when I told her about my defensive walls with Tom and said that often over the years she had felt set in stone herself, not daring to move, in case she gave something away.

She said she knew that I had felt this as coldness, but she hadn't dared to try and explain in case she broke her promise. She admitted that she was also afraid that Dodo might reveal the truth at any time. At least that is one benefit from this volcanic eruption in our lives: the truth is out, so we can all start to move more freely again.

Dodo has put her house in Oxford onto the market and is renting a place near us in Caldbeck. I am not sure she will survive very long so deep in the fells and so far away from the bright lights of Oxford and London, but she aims to try and she can always volunteer at the Theatre by the Lake in Keswick. Lots of exciting things going on there.

We have told Jez and Josh about Dodo's new status, but they seem disposed to add her to their pantheon rather than displace Kay and Cliff, which is a relief to all of us. I suppose, in this era of reconstituted families, it is not so hard to assimilate an extra granny. Maybe they will have three, if the Lady Edith ever manages to bestir herself. Tom is trying to re-connect with her, but he has not had much luck so far, despite the success of the gala night, which she refers to as a triumph – for herself, of course.

Jez and Josh are the ones keeping us all going, with their matter-of-fact acceptance of it all. I suppose there are undoubted benefits to having Dodo so near, with her network of contacts in the media world, but they are surprisingly keen on working alongside her on the renovation of her Caldbeck cottage. I am having to reassess my opinion of my mother as she is proving adept at some very practical tasks, such as decorating, putting up shelves, and even plastering. The knock-on effect on Jez is amazing – she has taken to a shapeless boiler suit and a dripping paintbrush as to the manor born.

I have legally become Meg and am trying out a different incarnation, which involves a green streak in my hair and a lot more trips down to London. I am thinking about taking a sabbatical and exploring Eastern Europe – Prague of course will be a key destination and Dodo will be my tour guide.

Tom is not scared of me packing my bags anymore. He is travelling himself, writing a book called *Diplomatic Children: The Cost*. Kay is helping him with the research and they hope to involve Lady Edith, if she can be bothered. He has made the box room into a study and bought a big old-fashioned oak desk with a green leather top and two rows of pigeon-holes. It is under the window that looks out towards the fells.

I have laminated my Latin motto for him and stuck it up above the desk. We have jointly adopted it as the way forward –

me in the outer world and he in the inner. *Ambulando Solvitur.* It looks very businesslike.

One last point: Dodo was on her way back to the house not for a great reunion but because she had forgotten her purse. Sometimes I amuse myself with how the conversation might have gone if she had not taken the bend too fast...

Acknowledgements

Extracts from *Marina* and *The Waste Land* by T S Eliot used with permission of Faber & Faber.

Author's Note

For Jungian sandplay therapists who might be concerned about confidentiality issues, the sand trays are based solely on my own authentic process over a period of eighteen months. The intriguing truth is that, in the process of writing the novel, my unconscious has spun a completely new tale to make sense of the same figures in the sand.

32534827R00096

Printed in Poland
by Amazon Fulfillment
Poland Sp. z o.o., Wrocław